RULE 34

VOLUME 1

WEIRD AND WONDERFUL FETISH EROTICA

Edited by
Zak Jane Keir

www.sincyrpublishing.com
sincyr.submissions@gmail.com

Compilation Copyright © 2019 SinCyr Publishing, University Place, WA 98466, reprinted from Sexy Little Pages © 2017

Pressure Points Copyright © 2017 VK Foxe
Anonymous Copyright © 2017 Elna Holst
Cheap Meat Copyright © 2017 Charlie Powell
And Eddie Still Makes Three Copyright © 2017 Zak Jane Keir
Tell Me When It Hurts Copyright © 2017 Elizabeth Coldwell
Cancel Job Copyright © 2017 Alain Bell
Fire Copyright © 2017 Lisabet Sarai
Ring My Bell Copyright © 2017 Dylan McEwan
Soft Copyright © 2017 Sonni de Soto
Chasmophilia Copyright © 2017 Arden de Winter

All rights reserved. No part of this publication may be reproduced, distributed or transmitted in any form or by any means, without prior written permission. This is a work of fiction. Names, characters, places, and incidents are a product of the author's imagination. Locales and public names are sometimes used for atmospheric purposes. Any resemblance to actual people, living or dead, or to businesses, companies, events, institutions, or locales is completely coincidental. All characters are above the age of 18. All trademarks and wordmarks used in this collection of fiction are the property of their respective owners.

This is a former Sexy Little Pages publication and does not follow SinCyr Publishing's strict consent requirements.

Layout by Sexy Little Pages

Print ISBN: 978-1-948780-24-7

CONTENTS

PRESSURE POINTS by VK Foxe 1
ANONYMOUS by Elna Holst 21
CHEAP MEAT by Charlie Powell 34
AND EDDIE STILL MAKES THREE
by Zak Jane Keir 46
TELL ME WHEN IT HURTS by Elizabeth Coldwell . 59
CANCEL JOB by Alain Bell 71
FIRE by Lisabet Sarai 87
RING MY BELL by Dylan McEwan 104
SOFT by Sonni de Soto 125
CHASMOPHILIA by Arden de Winter 146
MORE ABOUT SINCYR PUBLISHING 164

PRESSURE POINTS
by VK Foxe

MY SEXUAL AWAKENING started with Spock. When he did that Vulcan Neck Pinch I discovered my clitoris. I wanted to be conquered, overwhelmed by anyone who could touch me like Spock would. The neck is a very tender area and so made for an obvious starting point for what I thought of vaguely as "vulnerable patches." Until I heard some guys pretend fighting, and one shouted, "I hit your pressure point! You're dead!" I experienced a wave of temptation, so strong it made me dizzy, to march straight over, knock him to the ground, and sit on his face (that didn't mean the same thing for me then) until, in utter desperation, he'd *actually* try to hit me in a pressure point. But he was a jerk, and I didn't want to waste my do-whatever-you-want-to-me moment on him.

While I'm fortunate that teendom didn't last forever, it began to seem like that only applies to women. Out in the real world, I dated some *boys*. As if telling a relative stranger about your weird little fantasies wasn't hard enough. One didn't even want to go down (really, bro?)

and another was too modern to even put his hand on my throat. Newsflash: you're not being anti-feminist if she's giving you consent to be rough in the bedroom! I blame porn: everyone thought it would turn men into rape-monsters, but instead it turned them into literal wankers. I'd join them, but my fetish is so hands-on physical, it's no use. Why is it so hard to get some specifically inappropriate touching?

I did manage to score a hot-but-gay roommate, because sexual frustration is my state of being. Brian's at least an adult, easy to talk to. He also walks around without a shirt on, an image I store for when I'm jabbing myself with a knitting needle (too blunt to penetrate but long enough to reach anywhere I want to poke) and masturbating.

"Jess-jess," he asked, one night, returning from the gym to discover me home too early, "what happened to Taylor?"

"I canceled the date. He's boring." Taylor hadn't read a book in a year, a sign of an incurious mind, and a warning sign of bedroom stagnation. We'd done it twice, missionary start to (pretend) finish.

"He had a nice butt, though."

"Maybe if he'd talked out of it, I wouldn't have noticed how boring he was."

"So mean, Jess-rika," Brian teased. As I happened to stretch he reached over and poked me playfully in the belly button. My whole body responded, unmistakably: ragged breath, eyes going submissive-soft, and of course

I flushed bright red in response to having been sorta outed. Brian was, for once, at a loss for words.

I shook my head, tried to clear the desire to jump him, and gave a fake little half-laugh. "Caught me by surprise."

"Jessica, seriously, I'm sorry if I—"

"Whatever. That's just what I'm talking about, though. You're better, with a casual finger, than Taylor was with his most-of-a-hard-on."

"Didn't think I'd jabbed you *that* hard."

Maybe it was the rush of submissiveness, but I felt like confessing. "It wasn't that hard, I'm just... into that."

"What? Dough-boying?" Then we laughed like idiots.

"Seriously, I have a thing for being kinda *poked* during sex."

"Isn't that what sex is?"

"Poked *more*, with fingers. In my neck, under the ribs, and in random pressure points. It's weird, and hard to even to bring up." Despite my blush, telling him didn't feel terrible. Brian was easy to be vulnerable with, and I wondered why I hadn't done this sooner. He'd talked about his hopeless penchant for falling madly in love with straight guys.

"Sounds like a BDSM thing. Have you tried working the problem backwards? Go on one of those alternative sites, start with a guy already into fetish stuff."

***

Being a girl on a fetish dating site is weird. I could generously call myself an eight, with an unmemorable face and dubious feelings about my body (derived mostly from attempts to find jeans that fit a girl with a real girl butt). With the skewed gender ratio, a maybe-eight (see: awkward-smile selfie) under thirty years old becomes a four-alarm-fire red-alert-captain (relative) TEN.

Boys remain stupid. If I could trade dick-pics for secrets, I would blackmail the world. There were sixty-year-olds offering to sugar me and total douches offering to enslave me or something. Also, if typing "you" is too much effort, how will you manage to satisfy me in bed?

I ignored incoming mail and went through the profiles. Yes, even the ones without photos. UselessMitt had a sensibly written profile about being a switch and his love of bondage, confessing relative inexperience but offering an ability to listen. A guy actually wrote about listening? How ugly was he? I kept reading, though. Mitt had a paragraph about control being the fetish most of us share (hmm, maybe true), concluding: "You can be weird, too. We can talk secret fantasies and I won't tell, pinky swear." A good line for a girl with a finger-related fetish.

Cody (his real name) wasn't ugly. I wouldn't complain if Brian directed him to a gym, but he was nice enough, and the fetishy possibilities gave him an edge. I couldn't tell if he was funny because he was so freaking nervous, kept saying he couldn't believe I'd contacted him. I finally confessed to a non-standard fetish, and he looked down at his plate and said, "I've got a kinda weird thing, too. More like... a specific application of, of bondage." He took a deep breath and asked, "So... do you want to tell me?"

What, spill it just like that, here in the restaurant? I couldn't remember the last time I'd felt so nervous, but I'd come too far to choke. I took a deep breath and asked, "How about an introductory question?"

"Okay."

"If you know I'm into it, would you be willing to grab me by the throat?"

He blinked, maybe waiting for more. "Sure. That's not even strange."

He even noticed it my sense of relief, gave a shy smile. I invited him home.

I went in first, to make sure Brian was wearing a shirt. "Hey Jess-imyte, how did the date go?"

Blushing, I opened the door wider. Cody followed me in, and I introduced them. As usual, I'd failed to mention that I live with a guy, but Brian made his gayness obvious. This included a faux-whispered, "Hey, he's pretty cute," as we headed to my room.

Actually, he was cute. I'd been sizing him up for hotness, but that was the wrong way to appreciate Cody, who was shy, and thoughtful, and had a nice little smile. We sat close together on my bed, with the lights low, and made a pinky promise not to share what was said between us. I told him how being jabbed made me feel my vulnerability. How I liked the idea of being *forced* to go brain-blank and just experience.

Cody had a strange look on his face when I finished.

"Wow, I totally get that, I even... Okay, here goes. I *love* bondage, but especially having my hands, like, balled into fists and bondage taped or saran wrapped. It's great being cuffed or tied up, too, but honestly, it's amazing how much more helpless you become when you can't use your hands. There's even—is this too much?"

"No! Keep going."

"There's even a variation, where I squeeze stress balls first. I mean, I've never *actually* done this, but I can't help thinking that when you're actively squeezing, and you can't let go..." He was becoming breathless, charged from the mere idea, which was oddly endearing. "I imagine my energy being absolutely drained, so that I can't fight whatever comes. And, um, I can't believe I'm telling you this but, part of the fantasy is that without hands I can't stop you from doing things to me that I don't even want. Things I'm *not* into. Forcing me."

That last bit resonated all too well, and I felt the familiar thrum in my body. I surged forward; kissed him. The central dilemma of our relationship made itself present immediately: we both *really* wanted to be submissive. We pseudo-struggled for dominance, but we both wanted to lose. Still, the clothes came off. Cody gave me hesitant pokes, playing at taking over. His unwillingness to master me, to make it fucking hurt, ratcheted up my hunger for those fingers to *dig* in. I'd managed to get closer than ever to living my fantasy, but it only made the frustration more agonizing.

We were too close for me to give up, but one of us had

to take over to save the night, so I did.

I grabbed his wrists as we kissed hard, bodies grinding with me on top. I slid my hands up, folded his fingers down into fists, and squeezed them shut as I bit into his lip. He groaned, his hard-on pressing against my thigh. Well, fuck it, at this point I had him revved. I could at least get a solid pounding. And hey, if he liked to be "forced," could I break the "give head to get head" rule? Taking charge had its advantages...

I spun around and *boom*, sat right on his face (yeah, I know what that means now). And Cody wanted it—fast as I moved, he had his tongue out, waiting. I grabbed his hands again, kept them squeezed into tight little fists as he worked to satisfy me. Holy fuck, he'd read up on what to do with his tongue but, more than that, there was his obvious desperation to please me. My orgasm took me by surprise, and I found myself squeezing his hands harder, which made him moan more, which... Yeah Feedback.

Since I didn't know what to do next, I kept riding. I enjoyed the ramp-up more on the next one, feeling wonderfully wet, sloppy, and a little bit mean. I got so into it I forgot to let him breathe as I slid back and forth across his face. The sound of his gasping desperation, when my writhing lifted me up off him, drove me right to the next climax. I pressed his hands down to his sides, leaning forward to stare at his straining cock. Next time, I decided, I'd actually have to use tape, freeing *my* hands to... slap him. Or something.

I took a third orgasm, then got off him. He flexed his

hands, and I grabbed a condom packet from my nightstand. The little squares came out attached to each other, and I had a hilarious idea. I tossed him one, watched his trembling fingers as he rolled it down his shaft. I opened two more, ignoring his questioning look.

Between the lubrication of the condom, and me three orgasms in, he pressed easily into me. In that indescribable language of bodies, I indicated that he needed to manage the thrusting. He wiggled a bit, then took hold of one leg, reaching his other arm to my hip, and started working.

I plucked his right hand from my leg and unrolled another condom down over his two smaller fingers. Too much room left. I pulled his middle finger over, bunching the three fingers together, and tried again. I smiled at how silly it looked, and let him flex, stretching the condom a little. All this while he rose and fell, working me good, and I liked how focused he'd become. I quickly did the same to his right hand. Now he was a strange, three-fingered creature. They were more like pincer claws, and somehow that excited me.

Guiding his right hand to my side, I pressed his index finger against a soft spot under my ribs, but I didn't order him to do anything. Even though I was dominating him, this was for submissive me. He didn't get it, too focused on thrusting and his own submission. What he did get was a body-wracking orgasm that made him suddenly grip me—just right! I felt a sudden rush of pleasure, and my whole body tensed and tightened, and then—almost...

Cody's grip loosened *just* before I got there, and in spite of the three orgasms I'd scored from his tongue, I felt absurdly frustrated, on the edge of that big one from the fantasy. I may have growled.

His profile had identified him as a switch. If Cody wasn't wrong about himself, that made him a greedy bastard. He never took charge, didn't want to take charge, and a month in we both knew: Cody was a sub. He started feeling guilty about it, promising that *next time*, he'd do the pressure point thing, but we both knew it wouldn't really work.

By vanilla standards, Cody was the best I'd ever had, no contest. When I revved him up and ordered him to *drill* me, letting him set the rhythm in spite of his "useless mitts," he delivered. I'd never realized it was possible to be so simultaneously satisfied and frustrated.

Brian had gotten me into this mess, so one evening I blurted out: "He's awesome, except he's not doing the one thing I found him for."

"Why not?"

I skipped anything covered by our pinky promise. "He's too submissive to—"

"Give you the ol' dough-boy?"

"Are we really calling it that?"

"Oh Jess-alina, you silly thing. So he's good in bed, otherwise, and even fun outside of bed?"

"Yeah, pretty great, and getting better now that he's less nervous."

"I'm just saying... If you don't want him, pass him on over."

I rolled my eyes. "He's straight."

"And you think you have weird fetishes."

"Wait a second," I said.

"What?"

"Your thing for straight guys, that's not just bad luck? You're actually attracted to them *because* they're straight."

Brian has a beautiful smile, and the guilty eyes only make him more tempting. "All that talk when I was growing up about the gay agenda. It would have occurred to me otherwise, but they kinda made the idea of *converting* straights sound so hot! The idea just..." He stopped, gave me a dubious look. "Jess-jess? What's in your head that's making your face so funny?"

"Cody's pretty cute, yeah?"

"Yeah."

"Would you like to fuck him?"

"I'm not sure *he* would like—"

"That's not what I asked."

"Well, I mean, *yeah*, I'd totally love to, but..."

"Let me worry about the but."

"Jess-ling, the butt is what I'd be handling, if..."

"Let's go shopping."

Going full dominant meant dressing the part: black vinyl skirt and velvety purple corset, set off nicely by black, wet-look gloves that went past my elbows, and shiny, black boots that came to my knees. I even bought more scrunchies so I could pull my brown hair into a tight ponytail. I wanted to look properly severe. I got more bondage tape and a strap-on starter kit, too.

Into our usual flirtatious texting, I indicated my interest in pegging him, soon, and that he wouldn't be able to stop me from doing it with his hands bound. Cody would take the unsubtle hint, arrive properly clean. But come date night, Brian was the nervous one. "This is crazy, Jess-zilla. I mean fantasy's one thing, but..."

"He'll have a safe word. We'll take it slow. Chill. Unless you'll be too grossed out with all my girl parts lying around?"

"This whole society is nothing but girl parts lying around!" He straightened my skirt; I enjoyed the feel of his hands at my hips.

I'd decided to hide him in the closet, so that he'd hear how I set the scene. That way, if it didn't feel right to him, he could stay there or sneak out. "Just don't forget your part of the deal."

"I know, I know. I just don't want to ruin anything. You got really lucky with such a cute one on your first try and—" A knock at the door. Cody had arrived. Brian swallowed hard, nodded, then went for my closet. I collected myself and opened the door.

He wore t-shirt and jeans, expecting a basic evening in. I watched his eyes go wide as I yanked him inside and shut the door. I'd had time to plan the scene, to make every action communicate my dominance. As he walked the familiar path to my bedroom, I had a hand guiding him, pressing him forward. I didn't let him do or decide anything, but pulled off his clothing myself: shoes and socks, shirt, belt, jeans and boxers, I took them from him, working slowly.

"Same stoplight safe words, but tonight is going to be different." Cody started to reply, but I silenced him with a finger tap against his upper lip. "It's going to be intense, and new. And it may be too much, so just remember that you *can* use a safe word. I will understand if you need to. However. I want you to take it. I want you to suffer. I want you to experience something, for me, that you might not like. Because tonight, we're going to get the balance we've been missing." I cupped his balls in my hand, fingers gently playing with him, as I whispered, "Tonight I'm going to *use you* to please me."

I could *feel* his desire as I sat him on the bed and picked up the bondage tape from my nightstand. He still wanted to speak, but knew better. I handed him a knitting needle, a long silver one with a blunt tip.

Even I was buzzing as I moved to the side, making sure not to block Brian's view of Cody's naked body. Maybe I was warming to this dominance more than I'd realized, for, as much as I longed to let go and *experience*, I found my own deviousness thrilling. I'd managed to simultaneously tease my best friend with my boyfriend's body while *already* enacting Cody's fantasy of doing things to him against his will—and he didn't even know it.

I wound the bondage tape around his tight fist, forcing

him to keep hold of the needle, his thumb pressing down on the head of it. I wrapped it *tight*, so the needle wouldn't slip, so that Brian could easy apply pressure, so that that pressure would be predictably firm.

Much like me, thinking about Brian in the closet, Cody seemed focused on something other than his central fetish. I picked up the other needle from my night stand, and smiled as I saw him staring at the suggestively placed strap-on, with the largest of the starter kit's three sizes set in place.

With an electric hunger humming through my body, I finished sealing up his other needle-clenching hand and gave the helpless hand a squeeze. Then I slapped his erect dick, with some force, just to see him jump, getting him accustomed to my new level of control, and that I was using it.

From the drawer of my night stand, I produced the medium-sized dildo. "Stand up, turn around, and bend over the bed," I instructed, and he obeyed. Even the sound of his elevated breathing was exciting. I lubed both the dildo itself and his ass, not being shy with it. I made him wet and messy. Then, slowly, I worked the dildo inside him. Brian and I had agreed that if he could take this size without trouble, Brian could break him in from there.

I reached my other hand up between his legs, pulled his cock straight down for easier stroking from my position. He moaned so nicely. Being penetrated made him nightstick hard. "Does this excite you?"

"Yes, Goddess."

"You like taking it for me?"

"Yes I do, Goddess. Please let me take it for you."

Behind him, Brian let the closet door open a little wider, to get a better view. I'd never seen my roommate naked, and I hadn't realized until now how much I'd always wanted to. The door still half-hid him from me, but I looked right in his eyes as I worked the dildo deeper in and out of my boyfriend. Then I gave Brian a seductive smile—and rammed the dildo's full length into Cody. He gave a sharp gasp, then let out the breath in a throaty moan, and I savored Brian's visible *wanting*. He rewarded me by taking a single step out of the closet. His hardness wasn't for me, but I admired it anyway.

"Hold that in. Don't you dare let it fall out," I instructed. I pulled off my black gloves, then picked the roll of bondage tape back up. I wrapped the tape twice around his right thigh, then pressed a strip diagonally across his ass. Kept going around the front of his hips before crossing back down the other way, making a nice little X that would help keep the dildo inside him, at least for a couple minutes. Again I looked back to Brian. "X marks the spot," I said, as if to Cody. I finished off by wrapping another double loop around his left thigh.

Then I spent a moment touching Cody's body, running my hand along his back, his shoulders. I tousled his hair, squeezed his forearm. "You're mine. Understand? You're ready now, and I'm going to use you." I gave his cock another squeeze, then positioned myself in front of him on the bed. "Penetrating you made you so *hard*," I said, lying back. Then I flipped my skirt up, wiggled forward, and hooked my heavy boots around his hips.

He couldn't use his hands. Oh, it made this part perfect. Squeezing his ass tight so that my toy wouldn't slip out made even his tiny steps to the edge of the bed more of a waddle. He couldn't guide himself in, had to slide himself across my lips and over my sensitive clit. To keep steady he brought those blunt-tipped needles down into my sides, just above my hips. With slow effort he kept rocking back, his cock working a teasing withdrawal, and forward, not quite making it in and rubbing tightly along me again. I didn't want to help him. Let the teasing make us both crazy. I tried not to shift my head as I watched Brian's chiseled abs. He approached with quiet caution.

Cody withdrew again, pressed the points down deeper into me, pulling back enough and—this time he slid in. Something about being already poked made this penetration so full and powerful. I opened to him in a new way, felt like I was swallowing him all up. It made me want to touch and pull at him.

I reached forward, grabbed his arms to bring his upper body closer, intentionally bending him over for Brian. I'd never realized I could delight in such a seductive villainy before. I'd forced him to reposition the needles all the way up to just under my collarbone. I could feel in the way his hardness *pulsed* inside me that he was straining not to let the toy in his ass slide out. My tape would only do so much, so Cody focused on that first, then worked, within the confines of his awkward position, to pull back and thrust in. I felt every inch of him moving inside me, as if I'd squeezed his cock in a third fist. And as he trusted himself to press more weight down through his useless fists into two points that jabbed my soft, vulnerable flesh, I dropped my hold on his wrists and just let the experience wash over me.

Except I had to do one last thing. "Are you ready to do what I ask?"

"Anything."

"Anything? Really?"

"Please."

"I want to make you do something you won't like!"

He moaned in response, whispered, "Please. Please, Goddess."

Then I said what Brian and we'd jokingly called our *unsafe* word. "Purple."

Cody gave me a puzzled look, then jerked in surprise as Brian's hands found his hips. "Uh..." Cody swallowed hard.

"You'll take it for me, won't you?" I asked.

Brian pulled at the bondage tape, slid it up higher along Cody's ass, and caught the dildo that slipped out. He placed it on the night stand and lubed up.

"Keep fucking me," I whispered. A combination of sensations took me up a steep, intense rise of sexual pleasure: the play of confusion and excitement on Cody's face, the motions and sounds of Brian lubing his thick cock, and the extra weight pressing down on me through those two heavy points. When Cody continued to obey me, tried to focus on thrusting, and I felt that his hardness hadn't waned at all, I knew I was right: he *wanted* this. No, he didn't want to be fucked by a man, but he needed to be helpless to resist my enjoyment of seeing him fucked by a man. The realization arrived just as Cody drove himself deeper than I felt he'd ever gone, and I just erupted.

I've had a few orgasms that lingered, but this one came with immediate aftershocks, as if the sensitivity had been turned up to the point that even the simple motion of Cody dragging his cock back out of me seemed like the most erotic grinding together of our most secret selves. I rolled through the waves of this extended orgasm so long that I missed watching the real show begin.

But I heard it. Cody's little gasps followed by a long, helpless groan sent me scaling back up Orgasm Mountain, toward the peak. Brian's grunt and the slap of their thighs meeting tossed me right off the cliff, or maybe it was how Brian smacking into Cody drove him into me with a sudden, insensitive recklessness. His upper body tightened up, dragging those points down to my breasts. Unable to focus much on balance anymore, Cody pressed down so hard that the ends of the needles caved in the top of my breasts. It wasn't a pressure point exactly, but looking down to see just how roughly I'd been jabbed intensified every sensation.

I looked up to see Cody's face, his mouth open, eyes pleading. His breath came quick and desperate, confused by his enjoyment. I bit my lip as Brian reached around him and, grabbing my thighs, brought us tighter together. He slid my ankles higher up Cody's back, continuing to pound my boyfriend as the angle of Cody's own entry continued to shift. He drove in steeper, with a delicious violence, crushing me with pleasure just by letting Brian's thrusts reverberate through him. I watched Cody's face as he took it, and it made me climax again.

From there, I didn't even have time to rest between orgasms. Time passed as a series of images, the way you remember things from being black-out drunk. Brian yanking Cody's hair back and whispering into his ear, "Tell us you like it." I don't remember his response, just that I was coming then, too. I know Brian kept up his end of the deal, directing Cody's hands, forcing him to jab me in pressure point after pressure point, but somehow I only have snapshots of my own straining in response. Which is crazy! *That* was my inspiration for the whole thing. We hadn't predicted how Cody would sorta tighten up, and lie so heavily on me that I got the jabbing for free, with his being overwhelmed.

I didn't miss the best moment: my boyfriend stealing my full attention with his intense look of mingled horror and ecstasy. He didn't want to believe he would do it this way, but he came monstrously hard, pumping burst after seemingly endless burst into me. I absolutely screamed as mine started, as if this last orgasm was a part of me being duct-tape-ripped away.

After what felt like a long blink, Cody lay beside me,

asking, "But you know I'm still straight, right? I mean, I am, aren't I?"

I gave a little laugh and petted his head, which took more coordination than I had, but was easier than trying to word with my mouth. Brian, standing above us, said, "Yeah, you're straight. I can tell by where your eyes go." He smiled gently and added, "True, with my cock deep in your ass you just came harder than you probably ever, but hey, prostates are weird. Don't worry about it."

"But do you feel humiliated?" I asked, finally able to speak.

Though already fairly flushed, Cody's face went a brighter red. "Yeah," he whispered.

Thinking about Brian's sticky offering leaking out of my boyfriend excited me, and I immediately saw our next position. I'd sit on Cody's face. His legs would rest against Brian's chest. Brian would hold the knitting needles.

If fetish desire, and being able to control it, could make my straight boyfriend accept being fucked for me, I wondered if I could twist things around and lure *Brian* into pounding me. The possibilities were endless.

Because it turns out I'm a particular kind of switch: a sub for the physical stuff, but a domme for the mental. I like being the web-spinner, the devious architect of erotic delight... and then I want to submit. Not to a person, but to the sensation itself. With Brian handling the momentary dominance, I could have it all. Everyone has their fetish needs, their vulnerabilities, and what could be more exciting than applying the right kind of pressure to them?

About the Author

VK Foxe is a F/m writing duo living the BDSM dream. They write erotica across genres, from urban fantasy to more straightforward subversiveness, letting the most exciting ideas lead the way. Their latest novel is Mistress of Mazes.

ANONYMOUS
by Elna Holst

SHE COMES TO ME when I have had a terrible day. This is not magic. I have sent her a text message, and my request has been granted. I need comfort, and my mother will not do.

Mother is asleep in the other bedroom—her bedroom—snoring. She is very fat, I think that's why she snores. People say I shouldn't use that word to describe her, it's disrespectful. But the disrespect is on their side, if so; I am merely stating a fact. She is a big woman, she is rotund. She takes up the loveseat settee, more or less on her own.

Let's forget about Mother—her girth and her noise. It is difficult, but I can do it sometimes, closing my bedroom door, opening the curtains and letting my walls and eyes bathe in moonlight. I sit in this monochrome glow, crept up on my one person bed, waiting.

She will keep me waiting for a while yet. I cannot say whether this is because it does something for her, to keep me in a state of high-strung expectancy, or whether she has a long way to go. While I wait, I like to dream up an identity for her. Tonight she will be the petite service clerk at the train station convenience store, who insulted me, repeatedly, this morning. She will fit the role easily, effortlessly, as she always does; her hair is already that same indistinct auburn colour. I can't wait to punish her *Muschi* for her insolence.

I shift on the bed. My body is humming, awash with memories of her. Each time she comes she wears a different mask—all simple, just different colours. Over the years, I have come to realize, though there are generally but a very few words between us, that they cue me in on her mood for the night. I am hoping tonight's will be golden. It blends beautifully with the golden tint of her skin, making her face a blur, like the squared-out faces in news reports. It makes me want to cuff her to the bedpost, to fuck her hard and ruthlessly, my whole hand slick with her, burrowing through her tightness as she gasps and spreads for me.

I shiver a little, just from thinking about it. We must be careful not to make the bed creak too loudly. Despite her snoring—or maybe because of it—Mother is a light sleeper. There have been times when we have been caught off guard, suddenly aware of Mother shuffling about in the kitchen, the light coming on, and we have had to freeze, my tongue on her clit, her hands enmeshed in my hair. Forced into a stealthy quiet, we wait like teenagers as my mother builds herself one of her monumental night-time sandwiches and gobbles it up, while all the time I have to swallow, surreptitiously, because my mouth is filling up with *Muschi* juice.

She enjoys that. I can tell, obviously.

One time, early on, when we were less adept at which noises would or would not rouse Mother, we brought on her heavy footfalls trundling towards my door, and my lover slid off me, her thighs slippery enough to make the action all but frictionless, and went to hide in my closet, like an adulterer.

I sat innocently on the side of the bed, in my frumpy nightwear, as Mother burst in, raving about a racket, about burglars in our house. She wanted to call the police. I dissuaded her, gently but steadfastly, and as soon as she was out the door, even before her steps had reached the door to her own room, I was in the closet, finishing off the job.

That worked for both of us. Still, we are more careful, these days.

I pick up my old alarm clock on the bedside stand—an inheritance from my unknown father. Its luminescent hands have hardly budged since last time I checked. I put it down again and go up to the window, peeking out, hiding myself from view by pulling across one of the drapes. I don't want any insomniac neighbour to catch sight of me. And to be honest, I don't really want to see her: which direction she might be coming from, whether or not she wears her mask on her way here.

Though she is clever, I know that in my bones, even if I have never carried on a casual conversation with her. I bet she would wear her hood up, her scarf draped across her mouth. You can tell things about people, after regularly fucking them for twelve years.

I have never seen her face uncovered, though.

I don't think it would work for me.

I really don't.

Tonight she will be Ulrike, as the name tag on the breast pocket of that rude little service clerk said, and Ulrike's *Muschi* will be mine.

I sit back on the bed. I can be patient, even when I am provoked.

***

When she wears her red mask, she likes to be treated with a firm gentleness. I usually put her on all fours on the bed, and work almond oil into every inch of her skin, until she has a sheen more glamorous than any Christmas bauble. Then I stand myself at the foot of the bed and part her *Schinken*, so that I can run my tongue all the way from the bullet point of her clitoral hood to the asterisk of her anus. It tends to have her orgasming in no time, but I press on until I'm good and finished. I love the multi-flavoured, intricate taste of her. It ranges all the way from the sharp tang of a well-aged sauerkraut to the overpowering, cloying sweetness of crushed and tinned pineapple.

She is sticky with perspiration by the end of my feast, her mask plastered to her cheeks, her lips swollen with her own bite marks. I wipe the excess oil off her with a towel, and put her in my old dressing gown, before I go through to the kitchen to make her a cup of tea. It makes my chest swell, those nights when I have worked her to within a millimetre of her endurance limit. It behoves me to put her back together when she has come undone.

I can be tender like that.

***

Tonight is not a night for tenderness, though. I have been mangled by the world since I put my foot across the threshold this morning, and Ulrike will has to bear the brunt of it. Spilling my take-away coffee over me. Telling me it was my own fault. Gawking at me as I was browsing the news stands, as if she thought me a common shoplifter; then topping it off with trying to overcharge me for my pretzels. I read the papers as well as the next person. I know the 2 for 1 offer ends at midnight—today.

It all went downhill from there. There was a signal failure on the commute, causing my train to run late. I was flushed and rancid with sweat, my feet aching from running in my square-heeled shoes, by the time I got to work. I hate fluster. I loathe tardiness and a less than pristine appearance. I was cross and edgy, imagining I could hear my co-workers sniggering behind my back all day.

Also, it was registration day, the administrative office of the university overflowing with first-time students, willy-nillying all semblance of controlled efficiency out the door.

I hate students, too.

From time to time, there will be a female one coming in, auburn-haired and golden-skinned, a first-timer or an exchange student, a mature one or straight-out-of-the-crib, and I can feel my fingers curl up on the keyboard, a ghost passing through me, freezing my blood.

But it's never her. How would I know? It's what I have told myself over the years.

Her body gives me no real grip on her age. She is too supple to be in her fifties. Not enough baby fat, I think, to be under twenty-five. Besides—twelve years. Impossible.

***

My favourite fantasy for my occasional midday masturbation session—which I perform cramped in one of the stalls of the unisex, my phone turned off so that Mother can't reach me, my eyes squeezed shut so that Our Father won't see—is of her wearing her full-face viridian green. It means I can do whatever I please to her tits.

I can think of a whole host of things to do to her tits. There have been times when they have been so swollen by the time she is ready to leave that she has been forced to stuff her skimpy lace bra in her coat pocket, because they just won't fit. I like to think of the coarse material of her top chafing her, reminding her, involuntarily working at her, all the way back to wherever it is that she lives.

But I also like simply to put her on my lap and nip and suck at them, harder and harder, until I feel her coming, without my ever having touched her lower genitalia. Oh, she will be rubbing herself furiously against my thigh.

Sometimes I push my knee up and into her, just as she is on the tipping point, for the pure sensual power of it.

She has a birthmark, to the right above her left tit. It is distinctive, which excites and terrifies me, in equal measure. It has made me ogle more than my share of low-cut dresses, revealing shirts, always searching, never finding. Even at church, which I attend dutifully every Sunday, mumbling my Pater Nosters, tripping over my Ave Marias, I have to close my eyes in feigned religious rapture to avoid staring at newcomers, evaluating their height and width, the particular turn of a head or an uncomfortably familiar gesture of the hands. She is there. She is everywhere. She is nowhere.

***

Sometimes she is Professor Q of the Languages and Literature department. She likes this role so much that she has given it its own mask, a white one, fringed with a filigree lace, tied around her head with a black satin band. I worry that it will slip, but it never has.

Professor Q is head of the Romance languages, an impeccable woman, after my own fashion (or, to be frank, what I aspire to), smartly dressed, lithe yet muscular, expensively perfumed.

Her scent always lingers after I have run into her in one of the corridors; bumped into her—she must think me the clumsiest clod in existence. One of these days I am liable to forget myself, ram her and pin her up against the wall, and find out whether she is as perfectly coiffed and cologned everywhere as her carefully-clipped curls seem to suggest.

I won't, of course. Why have Professor Q specifically, when I can have anyone, everyone?

My lover speaks French fluently. Then again, she may be speaking Romanian. I have never had an ear for languages. She warbles her foreign words, telling me secrets I can never begin to parse, while I treat her to the cunning tricks of my universal tongue. I am always respectful to Professor Q, down on my knees, an eager student hungry for the sweet nectar of knowledge. She is a lady, and deserves to be treated as such. She even has her own wardrobe of tight pencil skirts, salmon pink silks, and sheer stay-up stockings. I love the whispering caress of her nyloned thighs as she rides my face. No underwear. It would get in the way.

I am working myself up, precipitously, as I sit here waiting. I will forget about Ulrike, forget about my just revenge. It will not do. I must harden myself, nourish my spiteful spirit.

There are times when I have imagined what it would be like to keep her here. No one knows where she is, there can be no trace of me at her place, nothing to link us— two strangers, for all that the world knows. Not even my phone number, as we communicate exclusively by way of an unregistered device, one which I have myself provided her with, and which she invariably carries on her person, faithful to my instructions.

But I cannot keep her caged. It would destroy the

balance between us and, besides, sooner or later, I would become bored and unmask her.

Which would be tantamount to murder, or suicide, or perhaps both. The end of the affair.

What's more, Mother would notice the addition to the household expenditures. She would think I had fallen pregnant, at least—always her worst nightmare.

Do not trouble yourself, *Mami*. The miracle of the virginal conception has not been prophesied to happen twice.

***

Her black mask makes me turn off the lights. I let down the blinds and pull the curtains, stuff a blanket along the doorstep, until I have sealed off every last sliver of a light source, and we are stuck, suspended, in primordial dark. She takes off her mask.

I cannot see it (of course), but my ears are pricked and honed in on the sound, the swish as she pulls it up and off her head, the clatter as she drops it among the knick-knacks on my chest of drawers. She does that on purpose. She wants me to know.

I move towards the sound. I have no other bearings, though I should know this room like the back of my hand. It's a weakness of my brain, a birth defect—I don't know: I am helpless in the dark. Without visual cues, I cannot make sense of my surroundings. I move through the black unknown slowly, staggeringly, as if the air had become viscous with the absence of light. This is her domain.

She waits for me by the bed. I feel as if she is watching me, inwardly laughing at me, though she couldn't; no one can see in this dark. By the time I reach my destination I am sweaty, shaking, my pulse throbbing with trepidation.

"Sit," she says, and I have learnt to trust this monosyllable implicitly. I sit, and she is right, every time: I land on the bedside, my nerve ends tickling, my body tense and awkward from this leap of faith.

"*Schatz*," she murmurs. I stretch my hands out, groping through the air, until I find her, a warm presence, a sinewy arm or leg. I follow it up the length of her, kneading as if I was handling a piece of dough, a chunk of wet and unformed clay, which my fingers could turn into anything.

She trembles beneath my touch. I tremble, too. There is a strange closeness in the unseeing.

When I have come as far as her shoulders we are usually both lying on the bed, each part I have touched of hers pressing against the corresponding part of myself, as if we were melting together, as if the darkness was quite literally blurring our outlines, stripping away our individual contexts.

She pulls me into her. She is soft and warm and gooey. I draw a breath and she sighs. My heart hammers against her rib cage.

"Touch me," she says, and I place the pads of my fingers on her cheeks. She reaches down to find me.

"Feel me," she urges, and I trace the naked outlines of her face, as she mirrors my movements, parting folds and creases, caressing and cajoling, until I am cleaving to the palm of her hand.

I put my face to hers, blindly. My lips press against her eyelids, and I lick the balls of her eyes, trailing down the bridge of her nose, as I quiver with illicit excitement, with the barefaced nudity of her, in the dark.

"Know me."

I part her with my tongue. She splits me open. I think she says my name, or I say hers, which would be impossible, and my roar is lost in her, she swallows it up, she infects me, and we come together, unveiled, her face in my hands, her digits deep inside—and it niggles at the back of my mind, I must have seen her, a hundred, a thousand times, by my side, on the train, in town, brushing past me, in the park, at the supermarket—every day, in short, for twelve years, but I cannot, I can't put the pieces together.

**

My phone burrs against my groin, from inside my pocket. I don't need to look at it. I glide off the bed, tiptoe through the twilit living room. At the door, I hook my keys off their brass knob by the coat rack, forego my shoes. The stone slabs of the landing outside are cool against my feet. It grounds me. I walk as slowly as I can down the first flight of stairs, though anticipation is building up within me with each tread. There is always a part of me that fears that by the time I get down to the front porch, she will have left again: disappeared into the Viennese night, the phone disposed of, ringing futilely, forlornly, in some close-by waste bin.

No one. Every one. No one.

No name. Every name. No name.

Loves me. Loves me. Loves me not.

I am at the last set of stairs. A shadow stirs beyond the frosted windowpane of the door at the end of the entry hall. Gripped by a sudden rush, I fly down the last steps, and fumble ungraciously with the lock. I can barely breathe. My nipples are rock hard against the fabric of my shirt.

She pushes through the half-open door and into my arms, lands a wet kiss on my half-open lips. She smells of cumin seeds, tarragon, rain.

I look out into the street. It has begun to rain.

"Happy anniversary, *Liebste*," she says in her broken German, and I look at her, finally, dreading, as ever, but yes, she is wearing a mask. It's chequered, harlequin-style. A new one.

"Who am I?" she asks, a smile playing just beneath the black-and-white.

"Ulrike," I say, and she cocks her head to the side, considering.

"You are upset," she says, and I nod, though it isn't a question.

She leans in and catches my earlobe between her teeth. She bites, hard enough to make me yowl in surprise, to make my anger flare up and rekindle.

"I am Ulrike," she says, and all trace of her accent has

evaporated. "You better give me a good hiding. Though I should warn you," she twists my protruding nubs painfully through my shirt, thrusts her knee up and grinds me into the doorpost, "I will put up a fight."

I growl and she tears from me, my keys dangling from her hand as she runs up the stairs, quick and light as a fieldmouse.

I let go of the front door, inhaling the rainy night into my lungs as it falls shut.

Loves me.

About the Author

Elna Holst writes lesbian erotic fiction, reads Tolstoy and plays contract bridge. Her effusions have appeared or are forthcoming in books from Sexy Little Pages, Black Scat Books, Ladylit Publishing, Cleis Press, and Nine Star Press. She writes in the mornings, works in the afternoon, and plays at night. Except when those pesky holidays turn up. She's some kind of -oholic, just take your pick.

CHEAP MEAT
by Charlie Powell

SOMETIMES, I THINK, the things that freak you out are exactly the things that turn you on. If they weren't, I wouldn't be with Jim. Jim used to scare me because I'd heard he was dominant, and I was pretty sure I wasn't submissive, but then we got drunk together at a party and fucked anyway, and since then I've learnt both that he's dom in a way I wouldn't have imagined (less spanking, more humiliation) and that that makes me wet as hell (a mere "Suck this, you slut," and I'm drenched).

Once we established that our kinks were compatible, it didn't take us long to couple up properly—we went from meeting up to fuck a couple of times a week to me staying at his four or five times a week. He makes the best scrambled eggs for breakfast and he's bought me a toothbrush and a multipack of spare knickers to keep at his. He doesn't even complain when my alarm goes off at five, even though he doesn't start work until ten.

Our incompatible working hours mean we usually save the kinky stuff for weekends. It's a particularly sweet form of torture, all those gentle, vanilla fucks from Monday to Friday, the flowers he brings home from the stall at Liverpool Street station, the way he gets up two hours before he needs to just so we can share breakfast before I leave for the day.

Food is a bit of a thing between us.

It's not that I'm fussy. I'll eat most things—meat, fish, bread, dairy, almost all vegetables, sugar—lots and lots of sugar—but if something has a weird texture, it makes me gag just to think about it.

"I don't get it," Jim says. "You'll swallow my come without batting an eyelid, but a salad leaf is tainted if it even has the barest smear of avocado?"

"It's hard to explain," I say. "It's just... slimier than I can cope with."

He laughs. "It's not slimy," he says. "It's creamy, and rich, and delicious. You're missing out."

"I'll cope," I say. "I like lots of other things. Chocolate, for example."

***

His mum serves prawn cocktail in avocado halves when he takes me to meet her for the first time. I eat the prawns as slowly as I can, praying she won't notice and that I might be able to offer to clear up, collect the plates and slip the avocado into the bin without anyone realising, but Jim is having none of it.

"Louise doesn't like avocado, do you, Lou?" he says, as I push the green monstrosity around my plate.

"Oh, you should have said, love" she replies, whisking it away with a flourish. "I'd have done you something different."

"It's not a problem," I say. "The prawns were delicious. I'm sorry I didn't finish it all." And I breathe a sigh of relief as she bustles out into the kitchen and the avocado disappears from view.

When Jim comes home the following Friday, it isn't flowers he's carrying, but a small brown paper bag, the kind you get from the market. He puts it down on the table, and I know what it is, even before he shows me what's inside.

"But I hate them," I say. "You know that. You even told your mum I hate them, remember?"

"Hated them," he corrects me. "By the time tonight's over, you won't ever be able to look at an avocado again without remembering how hard I made you come."

"I—"

He slices the avocado in two, scoops the flesh out into a bowl, and mashes it with lemon juice and olive oil.

"Take your top off," he says. "And your knickers, too."

He makes me sit at the table, head tilted back, while he smears his improvised mask all over my face like some kind of sadistic beautician. His smile is gleeful.

"Good girl," he croons, once I'm coated in the thick, green goo. "I'm so proud of you. Now, mouth open."

I'm not usually bratty—most of the time, when he tells me to do something, I do it. Except this time. On this occasion, I keep my lips pressed firmly together.

"Do I need to count to three?" he asks.

I shake my head. "No. Please, no. I really, really can't bear the taste of it. I'll do anything."

"But I only want one thing," he says. "I just want you to be a good little girl, and try one mouthful of avocado. It's not so much to ask, is it?"

I try to tell him that I mean it, that it'll make me throw up but the next thing I know, he's pinching the bridge of my nose and, although I hold my breath for as long as I can, eventually I'm gasping in air and then two fingers, covered in avocado, are deep inside my mouth and he's telling me, "Suck me, come on. Pretend it's my cock. Aren't you my well-behaved sub?"

It tastes disgusting, just as I'd imagined. But the being made to try it? The pressure on my nose, the thick digits in my mouth, the gentle, infantilising praise? Those things are almost enough to make me climax without him going anywhere near my cunt. When he asks me to lick his fingers clean, then lifts my skirt and penetrates me roughly with them, I come as soon as the rough pad of his thumb so much as grazes my clit.

***

After avocado-gate, humiliating me with food becomes a favourite game of his. I stop telling him when I don't like something, so he starts watching me like a hawk, keeping an eye out for every little thing I refuse to put in my mouth.

"What's wrong with the sausage rolls?" he'll ask at a party, as I neatly skirt the plate of cold pastries, heading for the sandwiches instead.

"Too greasy," I'll say, and then, as his face lights up, regret it immediately.

When he discovers that bananas are out of the question, too, he takes immense pleasure in making me fellate one, jerking his cock with one hand as he feeds the fruit into my mouth with the other, spraying hot jets of come over my stomach as I retch on the mushy, fruity shaft.

***

We're out for brunch in Peckham Rye one weekend when it all comes to a head. There's a little place we go to often, where we can read the papers, and linger over coffee and I can tuck into a bacon sandwich while he opts for his usual foul avocado on toast.

"Don't you dare," I say, as he raises a forkful of it teasingly in my direction. "Some kinks are better kept behind closed doors."

He laughs. "The weekend's not over yet," he says, and he winks at me as I roll my eyes.

***

It might have been an empty threat, had we not cut round past the new tripe shop on the way home. I guess offal must be in fashion again.

In the window hang dozens of the things, and although

they repulse me, I'm strangely drawn to their coral-like form, so much so that I linger as we pass, tugging on his hand to make him slow down.

"What?" he asks. He hasn't spotted them.

"Don't you think they're beautiful?" I ask, wondering how I can be so fascinated by them even as they make me want to recoil in horror.

"Prettier than you'd imagine a cow's stomach would be, certainly," he agrees, "though I can't say I find it particularly appetising. My nan used eat it with vinegar. I've never seen or smelt anything so disgusting."

He shudders at the memory, and then, suddenly, the corner of his mouth twitches.

"No," I say, "absolutely not. You said it yourself. That even you couldn't imagine anything more disgusting."

"Hard limit?" he asks.

"Yes," I say, firmly, though for some reason I'm still rooted to the spot, imagining running my fingers over all those rubbery-looking cell structures. Envisaging the weight of the pale, horrid things against my breasts, my stomach, my cunt.

Jim grips my hand, steers me through the shop door. He gestures at the man behind the counter. "Tell him it makes you horny," he whispers, bending slightly, his voice hot and wet against my ear. "He might let you have some for free."

There are other customers, incredibly. Other people who want to eat this stuff, I presume, who aren't there because it makes them wet, and squirmy, and needy as fuck. I have to wait in line.

I can't wait. I'm jiggling from foot to foot. I could swear my nipples are poking through the thin fabric of my T-shirt.

I have fallen in love. With tripe. With dog food, essentially. And, right now, I feel no better than an eager puppy. I'm practically chasing my tail.

I reach the front of the queue.

"How can I help you today, madam?" asks the man in the white coat, wiping his hands on the stripy apron that covers it.

My voice dies in my throat. Jim pokes me. "Go on," he says, as if I'm five. "Tell the nice man what you want."

I don't know what I want.

Because let's face it, I don't really want to leave here with a carrier bag full of tripe. What I really want is for Jim—or the man in the white coat and the apron, or any of the other guys who are currently in the queue, for that matter—to pin me up against the wall right now and fill me up with cock until this strange, sick craving goes away.

"I'd like—" I falter. "I'd like... one of those?"

"Honeycomb or thick seam, madam?" the man asks, and still I can't find my words. Even if I could, I wouldn't know the difference, though I guess the sexy-looking stuff is honeycomb.

I point. "Er, that one?"

The man looks as though he wants to laugh—I suspect

he thinks I'm here because I've heard this is the latest dish to serve at a pretentious dinner party, not because it makes me want to stick my hand between my legs immediately.

"We normally sell by the kilo, madam."

"Oh. Um, a kilo, then?"

He wraps it, hands it over. I swear I can smell it, even through the wrapping, and god, it's disgusting. What was I thinking?

It's the cheapest meat I've ever bought. There's change even from a fiver.

Cheap meat for a cheap lay, I think.

Once we're out of the shop, Jim calls me a "brave girl," which is when I really start to worry. I'd forgotten that he's tasted it before, so he knows what I'm letting myself in for.

On the bus on the way home, he trawls the internet for recipes, as the solid weight of the bag sits in my lap, tormenting me. At this point, I'd eat avocado every day, for the rest of my life, if it meant I didn't have to go through with this.

"So many options," he says, peering at his phone screen. "Raw, with onions, cooked in milk, stir-fried... It's a good job you bought a whole kilo because there are enough ideas here to keep you going all week."

***

"I don't want to eat it," I say, when we're home, the translucent alien sitting ominously between us on the kitchen table. "I'm sorry, I thought I could, but I'll be sick, I'm sure of it."

Jim gets up, and puts the bag of tripe in the fridge. "Come here," he says, softly.

He unbuckles his belt and tells me to kneel. He pushes his jeans and boxers down and lets his thick cock spring free, fisting it with an eager hand. He spits in his palm, spreads his saliva down his length, then slaps me wetly across the face with it.

"It's wasteful," he says, "to buy food and not eat it. You know that, Lou. If you didn't want it, you shouldn't have asked for it, should you?"

He waits for my response. I shake my head.

"Open your mouth," he says, and I do as I'm told. His cock slides between my lips and I moan. I love giving head.

He pushes deeper until he hits the back of my throat and I gag, saliva welling up around his dick and dripping down my chin. I whimper, louder this time.

"See," he says. "You say you're scared it'll make you vomit, but in fact, you love it when that's a risk, don't you?"

His hand closes around my throat. I can't breathe. It's amazing. I relax, sink into it, the way I always do when he dominates me like this.

He makes me crawl down the hallway to the bedroom until I'm on all fours in front of the full-length mirror. I'm soaked with saliva and pre-come and my eyes are smudged panda-black. Kohl-coloured tears stain my cheeks. "I can see what you liked about it now," he says. "You and that tripe, you've got a lot in common, haven't you? Both cheap as fuck, both pale and fleshy—" he squeezes one of my tits, hard "—both somehow ugly, but beautiful, all at the same time."

Tears spring to my eyes at the word "ugly,"—he uses it a lot, knowing it hurts me, but saying it precisely for that reason—I like it when he uses verbal humiliation to test my boundaries as far as he can.

"Fuck me," I beg. "Please."

"Like a piece of meat?" he asks, and I nod.

"Say it, then," he says. "I'm not fucking you until you ask for it properly. What do you want me to fuck you like? Like you're a nice, pretty girl or like you're a weirdly beautiful slab of meat?"

"Like I'm meat."

"Good," he says. "That's good. I need to get a mouthful of you first though, in case you taste as bad as you look."

Oh, god. I love giving head, but I hate getting it. I detest being the centre of attention. That's why it doesn't really bother me when Jim compares me to a chunk of cow belly. In fact, I kind of like it.

And so, when he lays me on the bed and ducks down between my legs, I keep it firmly in mind. So much so that I end up imagining that the tripe and I are one. When I close my eyes, I can almost see those honeycomb cells covering my breasts, my thighs, my arse...

For perhaps the first time ever, my head is in the game.

I don't try and coax him off me after several minutes spent staring at the ceiling, wondering when the anxiety will cease and the pleasure will begin. I imagine that I am offal and I let him eat me, and, miracle of miracles, I come, hard. From oral.

Jim can't believe it. He looks up from between my thighs and says, "Well, that was a first!"

"I know," I say. "I'm not sure what happened. But that was... That was... Nice."

"Just 'nice'?" he says, incredulously. "It's the first time you've come from oral, and the best thing you can say about it is that it was 'nice'?"

"Fine, fine," I reply. "It was bloody amazing, ok?"

The oral *was* bloody amazing, but the sex itself is better still. While Jim fucks me, holding my wrists above my head, biting my tits and my neck and kissing me like his life depends on it, I close my eyes and imagine that I am being screwed by every single man who was in the queue at the tripe shop, one after another after another, surrounded all the while by soft bags of milky, honeycombed alien flesh.

***

The following day, the tripe is still in the fridge. Jim takes it out, whistling softly to himself. My stomach turns. I thought we'd agreed we weren't going to eat it. Then he puts the bag in his rucksack, and slings it over his shoulder. "Back in a bit," he says.

"Where are you going?"

"I thought I'd pop round and see my nan," he says. "She loves a bit of tripe, too, you know."

About the Author

Charlie Powell has been an avid reader and writer of erotica since her teens. She has been published in several anthologies and is currently battling with her first novel.

AND EDDIE STILL MAKES THREE
by Zak Jane Keir

FOR THE FIRST TIME IN WEEKS, Jonathan opened the bedroom door, and paused on the threshold. Eddie gazed at him, sightlessly, from the pillow. Without really thinking about it, Jonathan had managed to pick the time of day when the light from the setting sun caught Eddie's empty eye sockets at such an angle as to suggest a spark of sardonic intelligence still gleamed there, even now. For a moment, the fact that the bed was otherwise empty didn't hurt as much as Jonathan had expected.

There had been a stage when they'd talked about taking Eddie out of the bed; putting him into a cupboard or something when the carers were due to visit. Noel hadn't wanted to, though, and Jonathan would deny him nothing: never had, never could. Besides, Noel had a point. The bedroom was already sufficiently unusual and, if they began stripping it of anything that might alarm the carers, where would they stop?

It was a big, high-ceilinged room on the first floor of a

small Victorian house, with a view of the park across the road. The carpet was black, and so was all the drapery on the big, high bed. The walls were painted a deep, purplish red—what anyone could see of them between the various pictures, the shelves of books and curiosities and the mishmash of antique furniture. There were a few animal skulls and skeletons; some in cases, some ranged along the mantelpiece. There were photographs of tombs and catacombs, some of which Noel had taken himself, over the years. There were quite a few sketches and paintings, acquired here and there, depicting variations on the theme of Death and the Maiden: some were reproductions of classic illustrations, a few were produced by one or the other of them. There was one shelf dedicated to various gifts they'd been given; a selection of ironic novelties such as vampire teddy bears and glittery Halloween decorations, and a couple of metal candle holders fastened to the wall. The one concession they'd made, in the final year, had been to put the heating on, after a well-intentioned health-care professional had started asking if there was a problem with the boiler, and whether they needed some sort of charitable or government funding to get it fixed.

Jonathan remembered what it had been like when the bedroom was warm. Oddly, it had been one of the things that really hurt, because it was such a pervasive difference: even more than having the carers, even more than the inescapable clutter of medical paraphernalia in the room. He'd tried his best to ignore it: every day, he would run up the stairs as soon as he got home, shedding his clothes on the way so he could approach the bed naked, ready, always erect. He could climb in with Noel and Eddie, and feel at home, for a while.

Towards the end, Noel couldn't bear very much in the way of physical contact. Eddie, of course, was unchanging in his availability, but there was nothing Jonathan could do with Eddie that felt any good without Noël's enthusiastic participation. Jonathan learned to control himself, content himself with a gentle touch or a merely verbal greeting, and retreat to the bathroom. Alone in there, he would deal with his raging erection, pulling himself off hard and fast, no lubricant other than the tears that spilled from his eyes and landed on his fingers and his cock, and all they did was sting and burn.

They'd met at university, just two of the relatively small goth/emo tribe in their particular year. Fairly early on, Jonathan had begun to realise just what he wanted from the small, fair, languid visual arts student who was at so many of the same gigs and parties, but he didn't feel anywhere near brave enough to say anything. Noel always seemed to be surrounded by girls, for one thing, even though there never appeared to be any one in particular that he was closer to. Despite the almost aggressively tolerant attitudes towards diversity, Jonathan had, so far, not been particularly inclined to come out. He'd had a couple of girlfriends during his gap year, after all— though there had been some amicable and enjoyable experimentation with other boys, shortly after he turned

19. Nothing really seemed a big deal to him, though; nothing seemed to have that curious intensity he craved but didn't fully understand, yet. He read a lot of what was usually billed as "paranormal romance" and usually marketed to a female audience and found that, while it was often trite, something about it resonated with him, even though it never seemed to fit exactly with what he longed for. When he began to want Noel, he fantasized about the other in what felt like a new way: it was never about Noel as anything less—or more—than human. It was kisses in a darkened crypt, or laying Noel down at the foot of some marble monument and gazing up into the eyes of a carven death's head at the moment of orgasm. Equally often, he pictured the two of them discussing mortality, perhaps reading some particularly fanciful obituary and a sudden flash of understanding between them.

It took over a year of occasional meetings—Jonathan was studying mediaeval literature, so he was never likely to encounter Noel in a tutorial or seminar. There were parties, though, and the student discos that set out to cater to those who wanted something other than rave or Britpop. Every so often, they'd run into one another, and there came a time where they really began to talk more. One or the other of them would bring up a news story featuring the Paris catacombs, or Kensal Green Cemetery's open day, or some more subtle and sensitive horror film they had both seen but few other people had even heard of. Usually, though, any such conversations would be cut short by someone else—frequently one of the pretty Goth girls who Noel appeared to find so easy to get on with—and Jonathan would end up going back to his own room and lying awake, stroking himself, thinking of things he could barely describe to himself, let alone anyone else.

Much later, Noel would tease Jonathan about the night they got together, and about his previous assumptions that photographers and painters never read enough books. "Took you long enough to bring it up," he would say. "We'd have had at least six more months of fucking each other stupid if you'd only mentioned the bloody book at the start." Jonathan always countered with the perfectly reasonable point that Noel could have just as easily initiated that particular topic, but there came a time when it was far too painful to be funny. That was when they fully understood how little time they were going to have, and the idea of having wasted any in the past became unbearable.

They were sitting on the same sofa, at yet another party, and they'd discovered that both of them took their Gothic identities as far as loving some of the original Gothic literature, and were well away on The Mysteries of Udolpho: specifically, the idea of the skeleton behind the black veil.

"Bet they were all having a wank over it, though," was the passing remark made by the girl climbing over them in search of more beer. "Wouldn't surprise me. Weirdos." Neither of them knew her, and neither of them ever bothered seeking her out afterwards, but they both remembered the comment because of what happened next.

"Well, I would, definitely," Noel said, and the look in his eyes made it utterly unavoidable: Jonathan leaned forward and kissed him, full on the mouth. He drew back almost instantly, terrified of what he had done, expecting a punch in the face or, at the very least, for Noel to jump up and abandon him. But Noel simply said. "*Finally.* Shall we get the fuck out of here?"

They fled the party, giggling, holding hands, but it wasn't going to be quite that easy. Jonathan shared a room with a quiet but good-natured law postgrad, who he would have felt guilty about disturbing and Noel had a nosy landlady who didn't allow overnight visitors. Still, it was early May and reasonably warm.

There was a little churchyard, apparently just a couple of streets away from the party, which had a reputation both of them had heard plenty about. Naturally, it was allegedly popular with various illicit couples, though no one ever admitted to going there for sex or even knowing anyone who had done in terms other than "My mate's girlfriend's ex did it on top of one of the tombs".

When they got there, though, after a meandering stroll with pauses for kissing in shop doorways, there turned out to be locked gates and a high stone wall. They looked at each other and Jonathan felt a terrible pang of loss and frustration, but Noel laughed, and pulled him close for another kiss. "See that nice dark alley down the side? Let's go down there."

Stone wall on one side and the metal fence surrounding the riverside park on the other, the town silent around them and only the faintest hint of dawn in the sky: it could be perfect, after all. There were more kisses, whispered endearments and encouragements, and then the touching and the stroking, the unbuttoning of Noël's black shirt, the tugging up of Jonathan's black t-shirt, the caressing of hardened cocks through tight black trousers and the easing down of zips. Noel came quite fast, a hot spray of creamy white over Jonathan's hand and spilling onto the pavement. Jonathan couldn't come, though he badly wanted to: even licking the warm wetness of Noël's orgasm from his fingers didn't do the trick. He felt close to tears when his uncooperative prick wilted in Noël's hand, but the other kissed the tip of his nose and said, "Never mind. We'll get it all right, next time."

They did, two days later, when the nice, quiet lawyer was out for the day. For the rest of the term, they managed to make the most of every opportunity they could find. It was going to be forever; they always knew that. As soon as possible, they moved in together: a rented room and then a rented flat, and then, when Noël's photographic career was really taking off, the little house they would share forever—as long as forever could be. They understood each other so profoundly that it didn't matter who was on top: they could be holding one another under the black silk sheets they'd bought for the double bed in that first student flat. Holding each other, kissing and whispering, sharing the fantasies of mausoleums and tombs, of dark, mysterious figures who had arcane, erotic secrets to share, their cocks rubbing together until one or the other said, fuck me.

Jonathan found Eddie within a month of their buying the house. At that point, he was the one who spent most of his time at home, as Noel was often away on shoots. Jonathan found himself endlessly enthralled by the possibilities of the Internet: browsing various websites whenever he needed a break from the transcription work he was currently doing to pay his share of the bills. After a while, he discovered the various Usenet groups dedicated to the more unusual sexual fantasies: discovering that he and Noel were not unique in their fascination with mortality made him simultaneously relieved and slightly resentful. It was late November when he entered "Life size model skeleton for sale" into Yahoo and, shortly afterwards, typed in his credit card number with trembling fingers.

The name "Eddie" was Noël's suggestion: a reference to the iconic emblem of a band they'd both liked in the days before they met and whose blokey, horror-comic trappings were something of a guilty pleasure to the pair of them when they were in self-deprecating mode. There were times, after all, when the things they did together had a gleeful, absurdist joy. Sometimes Noel would use Eddie's flexible middle finger to probe and tease the tight ring of Jonathan's anus, and the prospect of the plastic, bony digit becoming detached—and the need for a trip to A&E—would usually be mentioned by one or the other of them. On nights like those, Jonathan would frequently both giggle and cry when he came. They would prop Eddie up into a sitting position against the heavy oak bedhead, both silent witness and appreciative audience—so they imagined—to their fast, messy, frantic couplings at the other end of the mattress.

They always slept with Eddie in the middle, facing each other, their legs intertwined with Eddie's hard, cool, fleshless ones. The goodnight ritual of drawing one skeletal arm over each other's shoulder before clasping hands across Eddie's ribcage remained the same for as long as they could manage it. It was once of the reasons Noel had not wanted to go into a hospice, and Jonathan had promised him to postpone it as long as he possibly could. At least he'd been able to keep that promise, long enough for it not to become an issue.

Jonathan sat on the side of the bed and reached out, with a tentative hand, to stroke Eddie's shoulder joint. He remembered the night he and Noel had both fucked Eddie's face, taking it in turn to hold the skull's lower mandible to prevent Eddie's teeth closing unexpectedly on either of their rigid, throbbing cocks. Afterwards they had lain either side of their beloved, licking their mingled emissions from the planes of the skull, using their fingers to scoop out any stray blobs which had penetrated the eye sockets to splatter inside the vault. Even with this intrusion, Eddie seemed to be grinning more widely than before.

"I've brought him back, Eddie," he said, aloud. He laid the small, black box on the unoccupied pillow and stood to undress. The room was cool again, properly cool, the way it had been when they were happy together. Jonathan had closed the door on the bedroom once the officials and the professionals had been and gone, and slept—as much as he could sleep—on the sofa in the front room. Now, perhaps, he could be happy again. They could all be happy, once again.

As he shed his clothes, Jonathan felt his skin ripple into goosebumps, and licked his lips, feeling anticipation uncurl inside him. His cock rose and hardened, and he stroked it for a moment or two, enclosing it in his hand and using his thumb to smear the first dribbles of pre-ejaculate over the head of it.

He got onto the bed and knelt astride Eddie, leaning down to plant a kiss on the skull's even teeth. The light was fading fast, now, and he leaned over to switch on the little lamp on the bedside table, with its flickering fake-candle bulb. The table's drawer still held dispensers of lube and he extracted one of these before turning back to open the box he'd brought in.

Here was Noel. He was back with them. Jonathan caressed him, and kissed him.

In the days after the final diagnosis: not operable, not fixable, the last round of treatment hasn't worked, very sorry, counselling available; they'd talked, constantly.

They'd said they would be together forever; the two of them and Eddie, and death, real death, after only ten years, simply hadn't been part of the plan. How were they going to fix it?

"I could have you stuffed," Jonathan had said, one night, and they'd giggled and hugged, and elaborated on the idea, at length: Jonathan kissing and caressing Noël's failing body, and Noel responding to his touch, his cock getting hard enough for Jonathan to suck and lick. "Would they do me with a hard on? Would my dick taste funny when it was full of sawdust?" Noel asked, his hands twisted tight in Jonathan's hair.

They had seriously, genuinely considered it, until they found out the legal ramifications. They talked a little about whether Noël's body could be boiled and his skeleton returned but that, too, involved too many complications. Then there was the day when Jonathan came home from another long, dull but necessary shift of work at the library to be greeted by Noel calling from the upstairs bedroom, sounding so much more gleefully alive.

"Come and look, I've found it. I've found the answer!"

Noel was sitting up in bed, his laptop open, his eyes gleaming with the old, wicked excitement. Jonathan, having shed his clothes, sat down carefully beside him to view the website his lover had found. It was called Always Yours, and the front page displayed a range of dildos, plugs and cockrings, apparently made of silicon in a range of colours. Some were realistically phallic, in various skin tones, others more streamlined or shaped to produce different sensations.

"But I don't see-" They had a moderate collection of sex toys, acquired over the years: they hadn't done much with any of the toybox contents for a while, though. Jonathan looked at the screen more closely, gradually taking in key phrases: "special memories" "personal service" "designed to your specifications" and, finally "cremation."

"Yes. Oh, yes," he whispered.

Jonathan was glad Noel had found the website; glad he had found it in time, because a few days later, the final decline had begun, and even switching the laptop on would have been beyond Noël's ability.

Jonathan pumped some lube into the palm of his hand, and anointed his straining cock. He used the rest of the slippery, coconut-scented gel to coat the surface of the buttplug, made of silicon mixed with his lover's ashes. Lying across Eddie's pelvic bone, he reached up and pulled one skeletal arm down across his shoulders as he began to fuck himself. "I'm still here," he whispered, feeling his body climb towards orgasm. "We're still here. I love you. I love you both." He eased Noel in and out of his hungry, waiting, yearning arsehole, stroked and kissed every part of Eddie he could reach, and cried out, repeatedly, incoherently, joyously. They were all together, again. He could *feel* Noel, all of him, more than just the deep and delicious penetration that made his cock swell and throb, but invisible hands on his shoulders, the ghost of a kiss on the back of his neck, and it didn't take long before he was coming in powerful, explosive spurts, all over the bedsheets, all over Eddie, all over his hand.

He slowly drew the toy out of himself, kissed the tip of it and placed it in between Eddie's thighbones. He laid his arm across Eddie's ribcage and fell immediately asleep.

About the Author

Zak Jane Keir has a long history of writing about sex. Though she mainly focuses on fiction now, she has written for magazines such as Forum and Penthouse in the past. She prefers writing contemporary femdom fiction and also runs the Dirty Sexy Words erotica slams.

TELL ME WHEN IT HURTS
by Elizabeth Coldwell

SIMON HEARD THE CRACK as soon as he bit into the brownie. He spat the half-chewed mouthful out into his palm and saw a chunk of silvery amalgam staring at him accusingly, alongside the walnut that had reduced his filling to shrapnel. Despite the sudden, sharp ache in his molar, he felt his cock begin to stir, knowing he would be forced to make an appointment with his dentist.

It wasn't the usual reaction to such an event, but then Simon didn't have the usual dentist. Certainly, Dr Vesnina performed routine check-ups and, twice a year, she scheduled Simon for a thorough scale and polish, but she also provided, for select clients, a very special way of dealing with more complicated procedures such as fillings and extractions. He had originally found her following an enquiry in a chatroom designed for male masochists. He'd only half expected to get a response, even though he'd seen and read enough on the internet to believe there was no fetish so unusual, so singular, that no one shared it. As if to bear that theory out, a number of satisfied clients had replied within minutes of his initial post, telling stories of their own encounters with the good doctor. Their typing had been so erratic, so littered with mistakes, he'd suspected many of them were only using one hand.

Thanks to their recommendations, for more than a decade now Dr Vesnina had been providing him with excellent dental care—and some of the most exquisite sexual experiences of his life.

He dialled Dr Vesnina's surgery with trembling fingers, gripped with a mixture of terror and sweet anticipation. Svetlana, the receptionist, answered the phone after only a couple of rings. He briefly described his situation, stressing his urgent need to have the work done, and she booked him in for the following Saturday morning. The special appointments were always scheduled for Saturdays, when the surgery was closed to all other patients. Two days for Simon to sit and work himself into an anxious state about what was to come. Days when he had to fight both the nagging urge to probe at his sore, damaged tooth with his tongue and the need to play with his over-eager cock. Dr Vesnina was always very insistent that patients should not masturbate before they came to see her. She was a great believer in enforced chastity, and Simon was sure that, if she had her way, he would not be allowed to masturbate from one check-up to the next. He tried not to think about how unbelievably frustrating that would be, or how overwhelming the relief when he was finally permitted to touch himself. Those thoughts only caused him to harden further.

***

When he arrived at the surgery, hidden behind a discreet black door a porcelain crown's throw from Harley Street, Svetlana welcomed him inside. She was wearing a high-necked white latex dress that clearly advertised the fact she had no bra on beneath it. Her nipples, of breasts so large and firm they had to be surgically enhanced, pushed imperiously at the thin rubber. It was difficult for Simon not to stare at those nipples as she rose from behind her desk to take him through to where Dr Vesnina stood waiting for him. He had to stifle a moan as Svetlana walked ahead of him. There was no panty line visible beneath the clinging rubber and her tight, round arse cheeks flexed with every step. He couldn't fail to be aware that she was entirely bare beneath the dress, and the thought of how easily he might bend the pretty, doll-faced receptionist over her desk and just slide his cock up into her soft, wet depths had Simon almost fully hard in his boxer shorts. Svetlana would offer no resistance; she was as submissive as he. She would simply spread her thighs and let him fuck her till he came, the scent of fresh spunk and rubber heady in the small ante-room.

Of course, such behaviour was completely forbidden to Simon, or any of the other clients who visited the surgery on Saturday mornings. Svetlana was there to tease and tempt him into a state of extreme arousal, ready for Dr Vesnina to attend to him, and she played the required role to perfection.

Svetlana knocked twice, waiting till she and Simon were summoned into the small, antiseptically clean room. The dentist was busy at the small desk in the corner, checking Simon's file on her computer. All the details of his medical history and past treatments were listed there, along with notes that he knew were strictly for her eyes only.

"Mr Davenport, how nice to see you." Dr Vesnina's heavily Russian-accented voice never failed to send a chill of apprehension and excitement down Simon's spine. When he was a child, his dentists had been friendly, jolly even; always doing their best to put him at his ease and tell him this would all be over without pain or fuss. This woman seemed determined to do the exact opposite. She wanted him to be frightened of the gleaming array of surgical instruments lying on a tray by the side of the dentist's chair, and to dread the pain they could inflict. He could hardly be surprised. After all, it was what he wanted, too.

He studied the dentist for a moment longer as she completed her notes. A few strands of grey were beginning to appear in her black hair, and the faintest of lines were etched across her forehead and around her eyes, but even in her late forties she remained a striking woman. Her high cheekbones and small, tight-set mouth lent severity to her appearance, and she stared at Simon over the rims of her half-moon spectacles as though he was something she had scraped off the sole of her shoe.

"So, we're fixing that damaged filling of yours today,

are we? Right, I want you to sit in the chair for me, but first, you must strip naked." The faint trace of warmth vanished from her tone. "Well, don't dawdle about it."

This was always how it began. The ritual removal of his clothing; an act that served to emphasise Dr Vesnina's superiority over him. Svetlana had remained in the room, and the two women watched as Simon fumbled with the buckle of his belt. He never knew why, under these circumstances, such simple tasks began to trip him up. He was a successful, confident businessman, used to negotiating multi-million-pound deals and able to hold his own in the most stressful of situations but, under Dr Vesnina's withering gaze, his self-assurance never failed to drain away.

Shoes, socks, jeans and shirt were soon placed in a neat pile on the chair provided. Simon hesitated for just a moment before reaching for the waistband of his pale blue shorts. Taking them off would mean losing the last vestiges of his modesty. "Do hurry up. I haven't got all day," Dr Vesnina snapped, stinging him into action.

Pulling the shorts down hastily, he threw them on to the chair. He fought the urge to cover his cock with his hands. Already, it was standing up almost to his navel.

"Just look at that pathetic little thing," the dentist said to Svetlana, discussing him as though he wasn't even in the room. Simon knew the last thing his cock could be called was "pathetic"—he was bigger, by a good couple of inches, than any other man he knew, and at least one of his ex-girlfriends had complained that, if anything, he was too big—but somehow his brain was hard-wired to respond to insults and humiliation. Being belittled in this way only caused him to stiffen more, and a bead of juice to weep from the slit in his helmet.

"Now, in the chair for me, please, Mr Davenport," Dr Vesnina requested. "Let's make you comfortable, and then I'll take a look at that troublesome tooth of yours."

Simon did as Dr Vesnina asked, even though he knew the last thing for which her chair was designed was his comfort. Though the leather beneath him was soft enough against the bare skin of his back and arse, it was when she had the angle adjusted so he was lying almost horizontally that the refinements she'd had made to the chair kicked in. A restraint was quickly wrapped around each of his wrists and buckled firmly in place. Similar cuffs were used to secure his legs, spreading them widely apart. As the finishing touch, tiny padlocks were slipped into the fastenings of the cuffs before being snapped shut. Now he was going nowhere until the dentist decided.

Instead of the usual small, paper bib designed to catch spills, Svetlana placed a large, transparent latex sheet over Simon, tucking it around him so it moulded tightly to his body. A man with less self-control might actually have come at the moment when the cool rubber made contact with his erect, overheated cock, but Simon had learned from painful experience what happened if one of Dr Vesnina's patients came without her express permission. Even so, the little minx did her best to tease a swift climax from him, running her hand over his erection through the latex. He twitched in his bonds, his toes curling. It took all the self-control he possessed, but he managed not spill to his load.

The dentist studied him for a long moment, her gaze lingering on the contours of his cock, revealed in delicious detail through the see-through latex. Then she reached for a wickedly curved probe and a small mirror. "Open very wide for me, please." When Simon did as she asked, she quickly examined his mouth. "Ah, yes, I see the problem..." She pressed down on his broken molar with the sharp end of the metal tool, eliciting a wince of pain from Simon and an answering twitch from his dick. "Lower right D," she said to Svetlana, who tapped at keys on the computer keyboard, adding the information to Simon's notes. On weekdays, Dr Vesnina had a regular practice nurse to help her in surgery, but on Saturdays Svetlana performed the rôle. Simon had once enquired whether Svetlana was medically qualified to assist her, and had received only a contemptuous sneer from the dentist in return. He took this as an affirmative.

The extent of the damage having been determined, this was the point at which a local anaesthetic would normally be applied to numb the gum. For Dr Vesnina's Saturday patients, no form of pain relief was ever offered. Simon knew there were patients who underwent extractions without anaesthesia. In a couple of cases—or so they had claimed in the lurid accounts they shared in the chatroom—they had asked for completely healthy teeth to be pulled. He couldn't begin to imagine how much this would hurt, but he knew these men relished the pain and willingly consented to even these most extreme procedures.

"You know that I no longer offer the silver amalgam fillings, don't you, Mr Davenport?" Dr Vesnina asked. He could only nod, his gums packed with cotton wool swabs. "Now, I use the white composite. It costs a little more, but that isn't a problem for you, is it?" She smirked. "Many of my regular clients recoup the costs of their treatments with their dental insurance, but I can't see any plan covering the services I perform for a miserable little worm like yourself..."

While Dr Vesnina prepared the material she would be using to fill Simon's tooth, Svetlana amused herself by sprawling on a chair in the corner directly in Simon's line of sight and spreading her legs. He could see all the way up her thin latex skirt. Her shaved pussy, pink and wet, taunted him. He longed to taste it, to thrust his length up hard into Svetlana's hole, but, securely trussed as he was, he couldn't do a damn thing and the little slut knew it. She ran a fingertip over her folds, then put it to her lips, cleaning it of her juice. Simon writhed impotently in his bonds, the rubber sheet stimulating his cock unbearably. Much more of this teasing treatment and he was going to come. Svetlana knew that, too.

Just when Simon was resigned to suffering a humiliating climax before the dental work began, Dr Vesnina turned around. Svetlana immediately stopped what she was doing and hurried to assist the dentist, but her torment was immediately replaced by a fresh one. Dr Vesnina fired up her drill, its whining note sending a sick thrill through Simon's belly. This was the part he dreaded: the moment when she used the drill to scoop out the last shards of the old filling in preparation for the new one. Without anaesthetic, it was going to feel excruciating. Yet already his body was preparing itself to welcome the pain.

"Svetlana, a little suction, please." Her pussy-scented fingers now sheathed in a thin latex glove, Svetlana inserted the saliva ejector in Simon's mouth. He heard the whooshing gurgle as it sucked away the excess moisture he was prevented from swallowing.

Smiling cruelly behind her mask, Dr Vesnina began to drill. Simon smelled the burning aroma as she ground his tooth away; felt the exquisite pain in his exposed nerve. He would have howled aloud if his mouth hadn't been filled with the swabs. This was worse than any flogging that had ever been inflicted on his bare back and buttocks, worse even than the birching that left raised welts on his rear and made sitting down all but impossible for two days. Never had he come so close to begging the dentist to stop, to pleading for something to end the pain. He looked up into Svetlana's eyes and saw only indifference to his suffering. He didn't need to glance at Dr Vesnina to know how much she was enjoying hurting him.

As the vicious drill dug deeper, endorphins suddenly kicked in. Beneath the almost unendurable agony a dark, sweet pleasure built slowly. Simon closed his eyes and drifted into the welcoming embrace of subspace. Floating in a place beyond time, beyond bodily discomfort, he barely registered the moment when the drilling stopped and Dr Vesnina began the process of pressing the amalgam into place. Not much longer until the whole unpleasant business came to an end but, at this moment, Simon didn't ever want it to stop.

He was almost disappointed when Svetlana removed the saliva ejector and the swabs, then turned her attention to his wrist straps, unfastening the padlocks and then the buckles. She smiled, and encouraged him to rinse.

He took a mouthful of the pinkish, mint-flavoured liquid he was offered, and swilled it round his tender mouth. "Almost done, Mr Davenport," Dr Vesnina said as he spat it out and watched flecks of blood and composite material swirl away down the sink. The ankle straps were removed, the latex sheet that covered him whipped away. "I just need you to do one last thing for me."

She didn't need to elaborate. Simon was reaching for his cock almost before she had finished the sentence. He always hoped that, one day, Svetlana would be ordered to get down on her knees and suck him off, though he suspected the only person who ever had an orgasm on the end of her pointed little tongue was the dentist.

Fuelled not only by the continual throbbing in his recently filled tooth but by images of Dr Vesnina and her submissive receptionist rolling and grappling in a lesbian embrace, Simon wanked ferociously. The eyes of the two women were glued to his fist as it shuttled up and down his thick shaft. His breathing grew fast and heavy, and sweat prickled between his shoulder blades.

"That's it," Dr Vesnina muttered, "play with that puny prick of yours. But, if you spill a drop of your worthless stuff on my beautiful floor, I'll make you lick it all up, you useless wanker."

Her verbal abuse tipped him over the edge. His balls tightened, he threw his head back, and let a fountain of spunk gush into the air. With each jet his arsehole contracted in a sharp spasm, heightening his pleasure. When it was over, he dropped to the floor. He didn't know whether Dr Vesnina had been joking or not, but his tongue obediently snaked out and lapped up the drops of come from the gleaming tiles. He was vaguely aware of Dr Vesnina and Svetlana exchanging comments in Russian. He didn't need to understand a word to know he was being openly mocked. The dentist's laughter was enough to have his cock hardening again, but his time with her was up.

Getting to his feet, he gathered his clothes and dressed rapidly. Dr Vesnina took his hand. "It has been a pleasure to see you, Mr Davenport. Take care of that tooth, now. Don't eat or drink anything too cold for the next couple of hours or you'll really feel it." For the first time since he'd entered the surgery, she gave him a smile containing genuine warmth. He knew she took as much pleasure from doing a professional repair job on his tooth as she did from inflicting the pain and humiliation he craved.

In the reception area, waiting for his credit card payment to be completed, he saw a man of around sixty leafing through a copy of the *Reader's Digest*. The man looked up and caught Simon's eye.

"Abscess," he said, patting his lower jaw gingerly. "You?"

"Filling," Simon replied.

"Did it hurt?"

Simon nodded in satisfaction. "Oh, yes."

"Having this treated is going to be *agonising*," the stranger confided, in a tone which let Simon know how much he was looking forward to it.

"Good luck," Simon said, envying the man for what he was about to undergo. Remembering how Dr Vesnina had told him anything cold would cause discomfort to his recently filled tooth, and feeling his cock surge upward at the thought, he left the surgery in search of an ice lolly.

About the Author

Elizabeth Coldwell is a multi-published author and the former editor of the UK edition of Forum magazine. She was the launch editor of Erotic Stories magazine and one of the co-founders of the Guild of Erotic Authors. She is now an editor at Xcite Books.

CANCEL JOB
by Alain Bell

ANOTHER BOLT OF PLEASURE shoots through Ruby as the machine shudders and bumps against her clit. The rhythmic whine of the motors, gears, and rollers only adds to her arousal, which spikes with the barely audible thud that accompanies each jerk of the device. The slash of blaring white light across her retinas dazes her vision and increases the dizzy feeling of ecstasy. The chill of the glass against her compressed breasts provides a delicious contrast to the heat in her center. Even the slight scent of ozone and the woodsy smell of heated paper add to the mélange of senses that bring her closer to the edge of release.

The swish of the door opening behind her sends a surge of electricity and adrenaline through her body. Her orgasm isn't quenched by the panic of discovery. Instead, the fear and exhibitionistic thrill push her over the cliff, drawing an unexpected cry of euphoria from her lungs. The rapture flowing through her is greater than any she's ever felt. Her limbs lose their strength, from the combination of the complete sensory overload and the naughty pleasure of being caught in the act. She wobbles to the floor, her hands caressing her dripping core as she twitches on the scratchy and dusty-smelling carpet, lost in ecstasy.

The person who discovered her says something, but Ruby's too consumed with bliss to understand more than that the speaker's female, and stern.

After a minute, her ears stop ringing and her predicament penetrates her endorphin-muddled brain.

It's after hours at the office and, except for a pair of flats, Ruby's naked.

She's on the floor of the supply room, among ream after ream of pristine, white, photocopy paper.

And she just had an earth-shattering orgasm in front of another woman.

At work.

She's *so* going to be fired.

A different heat blooms on her face, down her neck, and over her bare chest.

The woman who discovered her taps her foot on the thin, gray-green industrial carpet. A faint whirring accompanies the impatient movement of the intruder's appendage.

A lazy tingle of stimulation flows through Ruby at the subtle noise, causing her sensitized clitoris to twitch in need. Confusion joins the fresh arousal. She's not sure of the origin of the sound, much less why it's such a turn-on.

Ruby stands, stretching to her full, Amazonian, six

foot one, her back to the intruder. All week she longed for Friday to come, then slogged through the day, anticipating her time with Alpha. Everyone should be out of the office, celebrating the weekend.

Despite her frustration, the blush refuses to fade. After being caught riding the photocopier, she resists the pointless act of covering herself. Ignoring the wetness coating her thighs and hands, she turns to meet the stern gaze of Julia Masters.

Ruby didn't think it was possible, but her blush deepens.

Of all the people to catch her, it has to be the woman who fills most of her masturbatory fantasies that don't include photocopiers. The same executive who is sometimes the co-star of the wet dreams that involve both Julia and the machines that make Ruby moan.

Ruby doesn't miss that Julia's gorgeous brown pupils dilate as her eyes lock on Ruby's breasts. The nipples, that were relaxing from their recent turgid state, harden and ache at the look of hunger that passes over the CFO's countenance.

Julia breaks the spell. "So, you're the one who's been wasting our resources." Her nose twitches and her irises somehow expand further.

Ruby inhales again, hoping the distraction her breasts are causing might be enough to give her time to think of an answer, and she smells what Julia must have noticed. The air in the compact room is redolent with the musk of sex.

While the room is small, it's still expansive for a supply closet. It has to be, to fit the ancient and massive collating photocopier that's mindlessly continuing its 1000 copy job. It's the only machine in the office that does a full sort, collate, and staple on thick documents and large jobs. Ruby's lust for the device is beyond her control. Something about its size makes it an outcast among the other, newer machines the company owns. While the more modern models can arouse her with their sleek lines and smooth operation, they don't have the same appeal of this one. The solid construction and sharp edges. The stamina to ejaculate pages, for hours on end.

And she would break any of those other, flimsy devices with her passion.

Julia's voice is deep and serious, but Ruby detects amusement, and a purr of some sort, coloring the tones. "At least you didn't strip and fuck the bank of copiers in the main office. Or are you responsible for the smear on the glass, which ruined the job I did last week?"

The blush that had been fading returns with a vengeance at the thought of her odd fetish. She still hasn't figured out why duplicating devices arouse her. She's sure it has something to do with the fact that she can be anonymously exhibitionist with copies of her intimate parts, but it's more than that. The simple sight of the alluring machines never fails to make her wet.

Perhaps not as much as the dampness that swamps her when she spies the CFO in her full, proud glory.

Julia wears a gray, woolen skirt suit. The jacket that

Ruby always wants to remove from the woman is absent. A blue cotton blouse is buttoned high, and covers any possibility of cleavage, yet isn't all the way up to her neck. Loose enough to not look inappropriate for the workplace, the shirt highlights her athletic curves. The color compliments her ruby-under-toned brown skin.

The flesh that looks so inviting, soft, and warm: Ruby has had a desperate urge to stroke it since she first saw the captivating woman.

Her skirt stops about two inches above one glorious knee and one high-tech electronic metal and plastic prosthetic. The sight of the white and chrome assistance device drives such a huge shot of arousal into Ruby that she wavers on her feet and, to her continued mortification, makes her so wet she's convinced that moisture is running down her bare legs.

Julia clears her throat and Ruby snaps her attention back up to captivating brown eyes. "So... What are we going to do about your... transgressions?"

The tone of her voice is chastising, but Ruby, hoping it's not wishful thinking, detects a hint of attraction in the honeyed words. The average height woman is nine inches shorter than her, but her presence dominates the space, making Ruby feel small.

Her crush circles her, studying her like she's a bug in a glass jar. A sleeve of Julia's shirt brushes against Ruby's overheated flesh as the executive approaches the machine behind her, the tickling contact sending another burst of warmth into Ruby's core.

A kaleidoscope of butterflies flutter in Ruby's stomach and her voice tremors, "I don't know, Ms. Masters."

There's a rustle of papers behind her and the sound of a button being pressed, followed by the cessation of activity by the photocopier. When Julia finishes her circuit, she stops; inside Ruby's personal space, but not touching. Her focus is on a piece of paper in her hand; one of the many copies of Ruby's breast compressed by the scanner glass. Despite the situation, a shudder of stimulation passes through Ruby at the sight.

Julia gaze moves from the copy to Ruby's breast, then she tilts her head up to meet Ruby's eyes. Small spots of color bloom on Julia's cheeks and temper the ice in her gaze. "No wonder you haven't discovered the perpetrator of the waste. I knew, the first day we met, that you were more competent than this delay in results would indicate."

Julia's words about their first meeting bring Ruby back to that day, about a year ago, when Ruby started at Rivers and Daughters Marketing. It was all she could do to keep from drooling when Julia walked in. The instant attraction was so stunning her ears rang, and Ruby missed the introduction to the gorgeous Chief Financial Officer.

Ruby's always preferred women, though she played both sides of the fence, but that was the first time with either gender that lust had left her speechless. Since that day, her panties become deliciously damp whenever their paths cross.

The CFO was sure of herself and stood proud in all her carriage, in one of her ubiquitous gray skirt suits and a salmon-colored button up. Normally Ruby would have been all about the amazing piece of technology that is Julia's prosthetic, visible below her knee-length hemline, but the woman stole all her focus. Julia's beauty and presence claimed the room. The shade on her serious and sensuous lips blended smartly with her clothing. Her luminous brown eyes captured Ruby's libido and have never let go.

Ruby snaps herself out of her reverie. "Well, yeah. I guess putting me in charge of finding the culprit is ironic."

The corners of Julia's lips twitch, and her gaze flickers with amusement, before the serious expression settles back into place. "Whatever am I going to do with you, Ms. Green?"

Lust clouds Ruby's judgment and she blurts out "Kiss me?" Ruby slaps her hand over her mouth, eyes wide, mortification filling her.

Julia's eyes widen and she inhales a quick breath. Her lips form a straight line and, eyelids narrowed, she stares into Ruby's soul.

Panic hops about in Ruby's head while she watches the gears turning in Julia's brain. Did she earn herself a lawsuit on top of being fired? Who says something like that to the CFO?

Julia's voice is ice. "To be clear, you want me to kiss you."

Questions join the terror bouncing around in Ruby's cranium. Is this a trap? What does Julia mean? Why does she need clarity? Does she want an unequivocal confession, like on police dramas? Is she also attracted? The hope of the last thought makes it impossible to speak as her heart swells in her chest, compressing her lungs.

Julia steps a pace closer, craning her neck further. "Just answer. Clearly. Succinctly."

Ruby comes to a decision. She's too passive in her life, despite her risky molestation of photocopiers, but that is almost beyond her control and she's as careful as she can be when she indulges in her fetish. "Yes. Please, kiss me."

Without pause, Julia draws her down into a kiss that sends stars blazing into Ruby's vision. Julia's lips are soft, and warm, and everything Ruby dreamed they would be. After only a few moments, Julia pulls Ruby's neck and tilts her head for a tighter fit. For timeless minutes they join in blissful heat. Stunned, and so turned on she's paralyzed, Ruby's arms hang at her side as she returns the liplock with all her pent-up passion.

When the pressure lessons, Ruby's about to object, but instead moans as Julia swipes her tongue across Ruby's lips, asking permission for entrance. Ruby gleefully allows access, and presses her lower body closer for the contact it demands, arching her back to keep their mouths in contact. Julia's tongue tangles with Ruby's in the classic battle of lust, driving them both higher, if the frantic nature of the kiss indicates Julia's ardor.

With a groan, Julia pulls away, takes a few deep breaths and says, "It's about time. I couldn't say or do anything for fear of committing sexual harassment." She glances at the paper in her hand before she lets the page drop to the floor and licks her lips as she caresses Ruby's breasts with her gaze. "Not a great resemblance when mashed against the glass. No wonder I didn't connect the images with yours."

Shock stuns Ruby. Julia wanted her? There was no sign of attraction until she stared at her like she craved to consume her. "But... I..." She shakes her head. "I had no idea. You gave me no signals. I thought my lust was one-sided."

"Well..." Julia shrugs. "I take harassment seriously. I fueled my masturbatory fantasies with thoughts of you, but kept my office behavior professional. I thought I noticed you checking me out a few times. And then, there were the times the lust colored your wonderful blue eyes. Those were good nights. But I..." An unusual level of doubt crosses her countenance. "I avoided any chance of impropriety, and let you take the first step." She turns her head away, her gaze catching on the copying machine before it returns to Ruby. A brilliant smile blazes across the face Ruby can't stare at enough. "Of course, I didn't expect to find you humping a copier."

Ruby turns away, again made uncomfortable by someone else knowing her fetish. That same embarrassment adds more dampness to her center. She wonders if her sex will ever be dry again before she continues her streak of honesty. "Yeah. It's pretty much a compulsion. The secret, dirty exhibitionism of the copies of 'naughty' parts. The chance of discovery. The copier itself." She runs a hand through her dyed hair, the unnatural, bright red color of her name. "I knew my discovery was imminent, but... I wanted one last fling with Alpha."

Julia raises one sculptured eyebrow. "Alpha?"

Heat and color bloom again on Ruby's cheeks. She wonders if her cheeks will permanently match her hair and name. "Well. It's a model XCM-Alpha Mark III Collator with Stapler. The full moniker seemed cumbersome, so... Alpha. They don't make copiers as sturdy and sexy as he is, any longer."

She can't believe she said that out loud, but something about Julia's discretion makes her trust the woman.

"Well. How about this?" Julia presses a finger between Ruby's breasts, her knuckles brushing the inner swell of her cleavage, sending sparks of arousal through her. She steps forward, backing Ruby towards the copier. "If you promise to never waste resources again, I'll let the matter pass. I'll give you one final experience with Alpha to savor. Once we finish, I won't share you with anyone or..." she points at the machine, "anything else."

Ruby shudders. It's impossible. Her most cherished fantasy is coming true. The magnificent woman she's lusted for, dreamed of, for a year, and the device that has brought her innumerable orgasms, together. How is she not going to make a fool of herself and come in seconds?

They reach the machine. Julia presses her against the hard, smooth, cool surface and drags Ruby's head down for another kiss. After a moment, Julia's hands disappear from Ruby's neck without breaking their connection. The rasp of a zipper is followed moments later by the swish of cloth against flesh and the sigh of fabric pooling on the floor.

The whine of a small, powerful electric motor precedes a thud as Julia's knee bangs against the machine. An epiphany hits Ruby. The origin of the sound from earlier is the prosthetic. It's the music of the actuator in the assist device, changing the distribution of torque when Julia's weight shifts. Fire burns through Ruby at the noise.

With a grunt of frustration, Julia kicks her skirt out of the way, from where it settled on the floor around her feet, and yanks out one of the paper trays on the copier. She plants a foot on it and presses her warm leg against Ruby's dripping pussy. Both women groan at the contact as wetness coats Julia's thigh.

The glorious pressure on her clit pushes Ruby closer to the precipice she's approaching faster than she has in her life. With no shame, Ruby grinds on the pliant, firm flesh while she plunges her tongue into Julia's receptive mouth and fumbles apart the buttons on Julia's shirt.

The paper tray emits a creak. Ruby pulls her weight off the leg with a flash of regret. "We shouldn't break it."

Julia groans in frustration, slams the tray closed with more force than necessary, and glances around the room. Her gaze stops on the stack of paper boxes. Ruby's silk blouse, dress slacks, and lacy bra and panties are folded neatly on a tower of boxes nearby. Julia swipes the pile off the cardboard, letting the things drop in an unruly jumble on the floor, and moves the top box against the base of Alpha.

She props her leg on the surface but, before she can re-engage them, Ruby says "Please, use your other leg."

Julia freezes: a look of hurt crosses her face and she turns her head, drawing into herself.

Ruby touches a finger to the CFO's chin and pulls Julia's gaze back to her own. "I don't have an amputee fetish. I promise." She kisses the shaking woman with as much tenderness as she can apply. "When I first saw you I was only peripherally aware of your leg. It was you, owning the room, taking the space, and blazing with beauty that compelled me. It's only later I noticed your assist device." She pecks Julia on the lips again. "I asked for your other leg for two reasons. Your confidence and usual nonchalance about your prosthetic is a turn on, and..." she glances at the machine she's leaning against, "if you couldn't tell, I have an electronics fetish."

Julia relaxes and a chagrined smile drives away the darkness that had passed over her countenance. "Sorry, but I have had... encounters before, with people who are obsessed with my stump."

Stroking Julia's cheek, Ruby says. "Shh. I understand. And I promise, if you had a simple prosthetic instead of that amazing..." a shiver tickles down her spine, "machine, I'd still think you are the most beautiful woman I have ever seen."

Julia stands straighter; her eyes open wide for a moment. "Oh! And when you first asked me to swap, you said leg. Not stump, or prosthetic. You don't think of it as separate from me. A deformity."

"It's you."

Julia places her prosthetic leg on the improvised step and jams it into Ruby's center with bruising force at the same instant she pulls Ruby into a teeth-clashing, hard kiss, tongue as deep as she can get it.

The cool, hard plastic grinds Ruby's clitoris against her pelvis, but the pain sends a lightning bolt of pleasure into her, flashing white behind her eyes. The first pump of her hips drags the bundle of nerves across the surface with a friction that further sensitizes the flesh. On the next pass, her juices coat the appendage and ease the discomfort to a sustainable and pleasurable level.

Ruby pumps herself up the incline of arousal while she finishes her fumbling task of opening the shirt keeping her hands from Julia's breasts. When she's done, she doesn't waste time trying to unlatch the lacy white bra covering Julia's pert mounds; just pushes the fabric out of the way. When she gets her first feel of the firm flesh, topped by diamond hard nipples, another flush of moisture further eases her sex's glide over the prosthetic.

Julia breaks the kiss, tosses her head back, moans aloud, and says "Harder."

Ruby complies, massaging the flesh and pinching the hard nubs between her fingers.

Julia's hips thrust, adding more movement to the grinding. The whirr of the prosthetic's response almost throws Ruby over the edge, but she resists, not wanting the pleasure to end.

After minutes of mutual thrusting, Julia pushes away, drawing a groan of frustration from Ruby. "Julia! Don't stop. I'm so close!"

The black-haired goddess shakes her head. "This is hot. Magnificently so, but I have to feel you. I have to fuck you. Sit your fine ass on Alpha."

Slack-jawed in awe that Julia continues to fulfill her twisted dreams of a threesome, Ruby doesn't waste more than a second before she hops up on the scanning glass, her juices smearing the surface.

Julia kicks the box to the side and steps between Ruby's legs. The executive presses buttons on the control panel, each beep sending a shard of pleasure into Ruby's nerves, pooling at her center and making her nipples ache as they harden to the density of titanium. When the photocopier discharges images of her womanhood, Ruby has to bite her tongue to keep from coming.

"This is your last bout of exhibitionism in an unsafe environment. Savor it."

Ruby nods and strokes Julia's face, wishing she could kiss her, but the height difference is too much with her splayed on the machine. Instead she sticks her thumb into the mouth she wants to kiss and jerks when Julia responds by nibbling on the digit. She doesn't think she'll ever have enough of the woman.

Her breath leaves her when Julia enters her with two fingers, her copious natural lubrication allowing the digits to slide to the hilt without pause. She watches in fascination and further lust as Julia's other hand disappears into her own panties.

Julia begins a synchronized stroking, filling and emptying Ruby's needy center while rubbing herself at the same steady pace. Ruby revels in the sensory overload surrounding her. The sound and feel of the machine. The smell of sex in the air, accompanied by the light musk and orchid scent of Julia's perfume. The sight of the fingers entering her own pink folds adds to the vision of Julia's succulent breasts half exposed in the open shirt.

Her breathing increases in pace with the speed of Julia's thrusting into her and rubbing of herself. Julia's breasts rise and fall in concert with Ruby's, her chest darkening with passion. Ruby holds on for dear life, wanting to come with the woman who is satisfying her most lurid fantasy.

Alpha continues its own metronomic shuddering and jerking. The machine is warm in its exertions, and the rhythmic flashing of the scanner bar under her ass strobes continual spikes of pleasure to her core. Page after page of the action of Julia's fingers entering her sex spurt into the receiving tray.

It's a losing battle and, when Julia's pace becomes uneven, Ruby explodes into an orgasm more intense than the one earlier in the night she thought topped them all.

She grabs Julia and pulls her close as she jerks in spasms. A moment later Julia twitches and shudders in her arms, an inarticulate, mewling cry coming from her lips.

Long minutes pass while they both pant, attempting to recover. When their breathing is halfway to normal and Ruby can talk, she releases Julia and strokes her cheek.

"Take me home," Ruby says. "I want to return the favor and show you that even with my unusual attraction to Alpha, I desire you more. You are more important than any fetish, and I need to savor you."

A stunning, joyful smile fills Julia's face, settling deep in her eyes. "Yes. Please show me."

The women dress in companionable silence and, before they leave to enjoy a future of mindblowing sex, and whatever else may come to pass, Ruby presses one last button on the copier.

Cancel Job.

About the Author

Alain Bell is a writer of lesbian erotic romances. Ze began as a game designer, a career that led to an enthusiasm for writing. Ze is passionate about LGBT rights and believes that love is love, romance is romance, and sex is erotic in whatever form it takes.

FIRE
by Lisabet Sarai

IT'S JUST A HARMLESS LITTLE QUIRK. That's what I've always told myself. It isn't as though I tie women up and whip them, or dress up in garter belts and high heels. I'll admit that my sexual life is a bit unusual. Idiosyncratic. But compared to what's considered normal, these days, I'm straight, red-blooded, all-American. A regular guy.

I do my research. I plan with care. I stick to derelict buildings, the ones that are already half-demolished by time and weather. Never any place within fifty miles of home. And never any place that's occupied.

All right, it's true that I imagine torching Manny's fancy house on Sycamore, whenever I drive past, but that's just a fantasy. And I know the difference between fantasy and reality.

It started about six months after Mom left. It was a thick July night, high summer, and my window was wide open. The smell of the smoke woke me, before the sirens. Wood smoke, seeping into my dreams, heady with recollections of campfires and friendly darkness.

My eyes flew open. A shimmer of electricity ran through me, like the heat lightning you can see on the horizon at dusk when there's going to be a thunderstorm. I sniffed, breathed in the message in the air. The smoke was speaking to me, whispering something sweet, something exciting, that I couldn't quite make out.

Then the sirens began to wail, blocks away. They came closer, their pitch rising. Something crawled up my spine and back down, then settled heavily in my groin. I threw on a pair of shorts and a tee shirt and made my way down the stairs as fast as I could on tiptoe. Didn't want to wake my father, that was for sure. The old clock in the hall said quarter to two.

The sky to the east was lit up like sunrise was on its way early. There was a strong eastward breeze, too, making the leaves restless. I ran barefoot along the sidewalk, the hot wind urging me on toward that eerie false dawn.

As I rounded the corner of Maple and Main, a spear of flame rocketed up above the trees. My knees suddenly went weak. It was the Saunders' place: Jim Saunders, who used to play poker with my dad, before. When Mom was still around. His old clapboard house was burning like tinder.

Something swelled in my chest. I could hardly breathe. I joined the crowd milling on the sidewalk across the street from the blaze, neighbors in pajamas and hair rollers, strangers in uniforms barking orders into walkie-talkies. I took no notice of them. I couldn't take my eyes off the fire.

Flame swirled around the two-story house, twisting and flowing through the structure like liquid light. The vacant windows filled with orange and gold tongues that licked away at the outer wall, gradually melting it away to charcoal and then to ash. It was terrible and glorious.

The flames drew me as nothing ever had. I craved them, wanted to feel their burning caress on my sweaty skin. I wanted to be consumed. For one crazy moment, I almost gave in to the need, almost broke through the ranks of police and firemen and threw myself into the blaze.

Something shifted. I felt the flames inside of me. They surged through my body, tasting my fear and my lust. They teased me, rippling up and down my spine. The heat was unbearable.

My dick went hard as rock. My breath came in gasps. I wanted to grab my cock and jerk away at it until the flames spurted out but, somehow, I was paralyzed, hands clenched into fists by my side.

I watched, fascinated, as the fire whirled and eddied through the shell of the house. I felt it circling my dick, searing my rigid flesh. I heard a strange sound, some animal whining in pain. I realized dimly that it was my own voice.

My eyes felt scratchy and dry, from the brightness and the drifting ash. I closed them for a moment, but the flames still danced on the insides of my eyelids. I could feel the fire breathing. It sucked up all the air into itself, then released it in scorching gusts. Once, then again, and again.

My aching lungs took up the same rhythm. My cock throbbed in time. The fire ate me from the inside out, turning my bones to embers, roasting my organs, bringing my spunk to a rolling boil. I writhed in its embrace, pleasure so acute that it was almost agony.

Thunder cracked, suddenly, close enough to deafen me. I opened my eyes in time to see the house's roof collapse into the raging furnace below it. A cloud of sparks flew into the night sky. Droplets of fire rained down on the crowd of bystanders. The first ones seared my bare arms just as the shock wave hit.

Like the house, I exploded into a million shards of flame.

I was seventeen. Like most kids that age, I jerked off a lot, sometimes three or four times a day. This was nothing like that. Nothing.

I felt light. My body had dissolved into light, into air, but air that crackled with delicious electricity. Aftershocks. My cock twitched and drooled residual fire yet, at the same time, it was as though my body was gone: melted and then vaporized.

I must have stood there, dazed, for a long time. A vicious box on the ear roused me.

"You little bastard, what do you think you're doing, out here in the middle of the night?" As usual, my father didn't wait for an answer. "What kind of trouble are you up to this time?"

He grabbed my arm and dragged me roughly in the direction of home. I went meekly, too distracted to struggle. I felt drained, yet my whole body hummed with lingering excitement.

I hoped that he wouldn't notice the damp patch on the front of my shorts. But then, what did it matter? Given what I had found, what I had learned?

Back in bed, I jacked myself off, twice, replaying the images of the burning house, feeling once again the seductive kiss of the flames. I fell into an exhausted sleep as the birds began to twitter. When I woke, I had a sense of peace and well-being that stayed with me for days.

The memories wore out in about a month. After that, I did what I could to recapture the dark excitement of that night. I went to see disaster movies, the kind where they blow up cars, or skyscrapers, or airplanes, everything convulsed in roiling fireballs.

I began to spend a lot of time in the woods. I'd carefully sweep the ground clear of pine needles and dead leaves. Then I'd build a fire (Boy Scout training coming in handy) and lie down beside it, slowly stroking my dick, hypnotized by the flames flickering and dancing among the logs.

I took to watching the local news every night, just in case some house or apartment or store happened to burn, somewhere. On the nights when I was lucky, I'd spend hours in bed, later, imagining it all: the awesome heat, the searing brightness, the smell of smoke, the crackling laughter of the flames as they devoured everything. My cock would be red and raw the next day.

Don't get the wrong idea. I wasn't weird or anything. I worked after school at the Kroger's grocery. I quarterbacked on the football team. When we were both eighteen, I screwed Lisa Downing for the first time, in the back seat of my father's Buick. She and I even went steady for a while. Somehow, though, we both cooled off. She was a nice enough girl, but she wouldn't have understood. About my secret quirk, I mean.

Three weeks after I graduated high school, I left home. Moved halfway across the state, found a place to rent, and got this job working for Manny.

I'm good at selling cars. I'm polite, well-spoken, and sincere, just the opposite of everybody's stereotype. But I know how to close a deal. I'm persuasive, Manny says.

Manny's got the biggest Ford and Chrysler dealership for two hundred miles around. New and used. He treats his salesmen like shit, but the pay is decent. I was particularly interested in the perks. I could drive any car on the lot, for as long as I wanted, provided I got the boss' permission.

I bought myself a police band radio, and spent quite a bit of my free time on the road. Listening for fire reports. Out here in the midwest, especially in the summer, we get lots of lightning strikes. From May through October, that's what I lived for.

I'd be driving along some country road, my window open, the soft night air ruffling my hair, everything silent except for the crickets. There'd be the crackle of static as the radio came to life. My heart slamming against my chest, I'd strain to make out the location. If it was anywhere within a forty mile-radius, I'd head in that direction, my breath already ragged, my cock swelling in my pants. Sniffing the breeze, I imagined that I could already catch the distant, intoxicating scent of smoke.

I was headed home after one of these night drives, when inspiration struck. It was just before dawn, late September, the fire season winding down. I was driving along an old service road that followed some river I couldn't name. Rounding a bend, I saw a rickety wooden warehouse perched precariously on the bank. Three stories high, sign weathered to unreadability, roof half-caved in.

The leaves on the beech trees that surrounded it were already crisped and brown. That would go up like a torch, I thought, if it caught a spark. Even the casual notion sent a bolt of heat to my crotch.

I slowed the car, stopped, gazed at the clearly abandoned building. *Why not*, I thought. *Why the hell not?*

I planned carefully. Bought the gasoline, two days ahead of time, from a self-serve on the interstate twenty miles from my home town. Borrowed a late-model Chevy sedan from the lot: dark gray, unmemorable.

It was a Thursday night. I made myself sit in front of the TV during the ten o'clock news, just like I always did. I was so wound up, though, they might have bombed the White House and I wouldn't have noticed. Finally, it was over. I turned out all the lights in the apartment, as usual, slipped out the back door and down the stairs to the yard, and rolled the car out onto the street. I didn't turn on the headlamps until I was halfway down the block.

My cock was so swollen that it hurt to work the gas and the brakes. But it was a good kind of pain. A taste of things to come.

By the time I made my way back to the warehouse on the river, it was past midnight. The evening was incredibly still and dark, no breeze and no moon. I began to get nervous, despite myself. My hands were shaking as I circled the building, splashing the gasoline onto the battered planks of the wall. Where there were gaps between the boards, I tried to slosh some of it inside. The vapors made me a bit woozy. The world wavered as though I had drunk too much beer.

Finally it was done. I went back to the car and got the fuses I had made of twisted newspaper. I stuck the fuses into the cracks between the boards, then went around and lit them all, with those big wooden kitchen matches. Each snap of a match echoed loudly in the quiet of the night. Each flash of electric blue mellowed to a steady gold. The sulfur smell prickled in my nostrils, and my dick throbbed in anticipation.

These days, I can't even strike a match without getting hard.

It was better than I could have imagined. Pure joy. After years of borrowing other people's fires, I had my own. There were no sirens, no spectators, no official types keeping an awkward eye on me. Just me and the night and the dancing, piercing flames. I lay down in the scrubby grass with my fly wide open and watched, greedily, as the blaze devoured the feast I had laid before it.

By the time the building had become a charred pile of debris, I was gorged and sated. I called in sick the next morning.

After that, second-hand conflagrations couldn't satisfy me. I have to have my own. I try to space them out, keep at least six to eight weeks between them. It's tough, but I don't want anyone to get suspicious.

The first few weeks after a session, I have plenty of memories to keep me going. I can close my eyes and recall every detail: the intricate shapes of the flames, the taste of smoke in my lungs, the searing, intimate caress of the heat on my privates.

I remember the sequence in which the barn or the shed or the deserted fishing cabin collapsed. Sometimes the whole structure explodes, or caves in on itself. Other times, one wall will totter and fall gently, leaving the others standing, as though buoyed up by the hot gases, until at last they simply melt away, crumbling to glowing ash. It is always fascinating, thrilling, enough to push me over the edge.

Sometimes, I imagine that I'm inside, during those final moments when the fire declares victory. I lie on my back, feeling the sparks rain down on my naked flesh, struggling to breathe as the fire sucks up all the oxygen. I know that it sounds a bit twisted, but I come the hardest when I think about the fire consuming me, taking me into itself.

Anyway, after a while, the memories aren't enough. I start to dream of fire. I wake up soaked with sweat, with a hard-on that I can work for hours without finding any real relief. I begin to get irritable, less polite, less persuasive. My work begins to suffer.

That's when I know it's time. It takes me a few days to prepare, and then, finally, I have what I need.

Last night, though—well, last night things didn't quite go as planned.

I picked out the place last week, a huge, ramshackle barn on a foreclosed farm sixty miles north of my territory. (I've found that reading the auction notices sometimes points me in the direction of promising targets.)

I arrived a bit before midnight in my borrowed Ford pickup. Lately, I like to spread a blanket in the bed of a truck and watch the show from there. Besides, the usual places I find my targets, a truck's going to be less noticed than a car, especially one that's a bit rusty and dented, like this one.

As usual, I dowsed the place with gas and lit the fuses. The fire caught like the place was made of cardboard. Sheets of flame rippled across the face of the building, waves of light so intense they hurt my eyes.

I stripped and lay down on my blanket, my dick straining toward the fire like the proverbial moth drawn to a candle. My organ was hot to the touch, fever rising inside me to match the flames around me. I fancied that it would blister my fingers as I stroked it, and smiled at the thought.

The screams ripped through my fire-induced bliss. Shrill cries, piercing the peaceful summer night, over and over. "Help! Help!" A female voice. Panicked. In pain.

My mind was still drugged with the fire's aphrodisiac. It took me long seconds to understand.

By the time I realized what was happening, the screams had stopped.

Naked, barefoot, I stumbled out of the truck and ran toward the inferno I had created. The heat beat me back when I was still six feet away. Beyond that invisible, impenetrable barrier was a brilliant wall of flame, stretching from one edge of the building to another.

The flames hissed and roared, but I could still hear the woman's cries, echoing in my mind. I was helpless, though. Darkness settled on me, guilt and horror so intense that my erection withered even in the face of my magnificent creation. I was responsible. I was a murderer. This was the final result of the obsession I had pretended was so harmless.

Then my luck returned. As if sensing the waning of my desire, the flames seemed to sink back into themselves. The heat lessened slightly. Then the lintel above the barn door collapsed, temporarily smothering the flames that had consumed it and creating a gap in the blazing facade. I seized the moment, took a huge gulp of air into my lungs, and dashed into the burning building.

In contrast to the brightness outside, the interior was murky with smoke. Now and then, the fire flashed angry red through the haze but, in general, it was surprisingly dark. I wouldn't have been able to see, anyway; my smoke-irritated eyes were brimming with tears. Fortunately, I tripped over something soft and motionless about ten feet from the door.

I squatted down and lifted the body to my shoulder, then backed out the way I had entered. Before I managed to exit, the back wall of the place lit up, piercing the gloom. A blast of heat struck me full in the chest. I scrambled out onto the grass, half-carrying, half-dragging my human burden.

Only when I was back at the truck did I breathe again, a long shuddering breath that felt cold as December. My muscles quivered from my exertion. I began to be aware of raw pain, on my chest, my hands, the soles of my feet. At the same time I noticed, almost absently, my cock was hard again, aching with that different kind of pain that I craved so much.

I smelled singed hair and burned flesh. Damn, what about the woman?

She lay crumpled in the truck where I had dumped her. Motionless. Was she dead? I held my seared palm over her nostrils and felt a stirring of air. Thank God. I relaxed a bit more, looked her over more carefully.

The few rags she wore were charred black, but I could tell that they had not been all that clean or intact even before the fire. Her feet were caged in scuffed men's work boots, which probably had saved them from being burned. She had wiry black hair, shot with gray, that looked as though it hadn't seen a comb in weeks. Her face was smudged with soot from the fire, but her fingernails were equally grimy.

A homeless woman, then. A hobo. (Did they call women hobos?) Who, no doubt, had decided that my barn was a fine place to spend the night. Damn, damn, damn.

How badly was she hurt? I could see several stripes of crimson on her arms and thighs, the outer skin completely burned away to show the spongy level underneath. Third degree, I remembered from Boy Scouts. Aside from the soot, her face seemed ok. Gingerly, I tried to push aside the shreds of blackened cloth that covered her torso. They crumbled to black ash at my touch.

There were more burns on her belly and breasts, but they were second rather than third degree. Blistering already. I should get her to a hospital as quickly as possible, I thought. Or I should get my clothes on and get the hell out of here.

I didn't move, though. I just watched her, watched her wounded flesh rise and fall with her shallow breath. I felt very strange. The lust was bubbling in my veins again, though the flames in the barn had begun to subside. I had bathed in the fire tonight, I realized, just as I had always dreamed. The raw patches on my flesh were the marks of the fire's kiss.

The woman moaned and shifted uneasily. Her eyes still closed, she licked her cracked lips. On impulse, I leaned over her and brushed my own against hers. My partner. My victim.

Her eyes flew open. They were a deep, velvety brown. The whites were a startling contrast to her soot-blackened skin. She focused immediately on my face.

"Who..? What..?" She tried to sit up, and screamed as the pain hit her.

"Shh," I told her. "Lie still. There's been an accident, a fire. I'll take you to the hospital..."

"No!" her voice was surprisingly forceful. She pushed herself up to half-sitting, despite the obvious agony she was experiencing. "No way. Folks like me die in hospitals."

"But you're badly burned. You need medical help."

"No thanks. I can take care of myself." She cocked her head to the side and looked at me carefully. "Who are you, anyway? You save me?"

A hot wave of shame washed over me. Save her? Nearly condemned her to death was more like it. "I heard you screaming. I managed to pull you out."

"You saved my life," she said flatly. It was no longer a question, and I wasn't going to argue. "I owe you."

"No, you don't."

"Yes, sir, I do, and I always pay my debts. But I ain't got much to pay you with right now." She looked ruefully at the few shreds of fabric that still clung to her limbs.

Then she looked me over, noticed immediately that my cock was huge, purple and oozing. She was sharp, no question about it. She gave me a crooked little grin.

"Well," she said, "there is that." She lay back down in the truck bed, raised her knees, and spread her thighs. "Come'ere, lover boy."

"No, I couldn't, I don't want..." I began. Then I realized that I did want it. I wanted her, wanted to sink my cock as deep as it could go into her fire-scarred body.

Last time I had a woman was Christmas, when I fucked Jen, Manny's receptionist, after the company party. She's cute, just slutty enough to be fun. All in all, though, it was disappointing. I couldn't even come without imagining that we were lying together inside a burning building.

Now, though, I wanted this nameless, broken woman as I had never wanted a woman before. I let my eyes slide over her breasts; ample, middle-aged breasts with nipples the size of grapes. I wanted to suck those nipples, then move over to tongue the blistering flesh around them. The legacy of the flames.

Her thighs were ripe, too. She was pretty well-fed for someone who lived on the road. Her black and silver pussy hair was as wild and tangled as the locks on her head. It was untouched by the fire, but I'll bet it reeked of smoke. I wanted to bury my face there, and just breathe, the smoke and musk mixed.

Mostly though, I wanted to ram my cock into her and fuck her until I lost consciousness. I knew she'd be hot, my woman who had lived through the fire. Her blood would be molten, her cunt would be boiling. I knew it would hurt, hurt us both, my seared chest slamming against her blistered belly, but she wouldn't notice and neither would I. We'd be too high, lost in the fire, flaming with the purity of lust that burns away the body and leaves only the bare, white-hot soul. Never, never have I wanted anything so much.

She wriggled her hips at me, raised and lowered her bum provocatively. My cock convulsed, and I nearly sprayed my jism all over her. "Come on! What are you waiting for?"

I turned away.

Something stopped me, I'm not sure what. Maybe it was the echo of that darkness that swept over me, reminding me that I was almost her murderer. Maybe it was fear, fear that the pleasure would not, after all, be worth the pain.

Or perhaps it's just that I was getting another lesson on the difference between fantasy and reality.

She wouldn't let me take her to the hospital. I dropped her at a motel near the interstate, left enough cash for her to hang around there and recover for a week or so.

Meanwhile, I came home and slept for twelve hours, as though I was in a coma. No dreams. No beating off, either. What would be the point?

I don't know what will happen next. Maybe I'll kiss this job goodbye and move to another state. Some place with a new supply of abandoned buildings.

I have an uncomfortable feeling, though, that at this point, abandoned buildings won't do the trick.

About the Author

I've been addicted to words almost since I was born. I began reading when I was four. I wrote my first story at five years old and my first poem at seven. Since then, I've written plays, tutorials, scholarly articles, marketing brochures, software specifications, self-help books, press releases, a five-hundred page dissertation, and lots of erotica and erotic romance—more than fifty single author titles including nine full length novels—in almost every sub-genre including BDSM, gay, lesbian, paranormal and scifi. I've also edited a number of acclaimed erotica anthologies, including volumes for the charity erotica imprint Coming Together which support causes such as Amnesty International, Planned Parenthood, and Doctors Without Borders. I have more degrees than anyone would ever need, from prestigious educational institutions who would no doubt be deeply embarrassed by my chosen genre. Aside from writing, travel is one of my most fervent passions. I've visited every continent except Australia, though I still have a long bucket list of places I haven't been. Currently I live in Southeast Asia with my indulgent husband and two exceptional felines, where I pursue an alternative career that is completely unrelated to my creative writing.

RING MY BELL
by Dylan McEwan

IT WAS THE PERFECT DAY. Not a single cloud marred the azurite sky as the gods blessed them with glorious sunshine. The absinthe and avocado shades of the short limestone grasses were broken up by the lilacs and pinks of the bird's-eye primrose and feathery bog-bean that flowered profusely here. They'd seen lapwings performing their spectacular, tumbling display flight, a tree pipit parachuting down from his perch on stiff wings, and a hovering merlin with his orange-tinted underparts and slate-blue back. The distinctive 'kronk kronk' call of ravens, the trilling of wood warblers, and the buzzing and humming of a myriad insects made a welcome change to the sound of passing vehicles, chattering voices, bicycle bells, lawnmowers, and children playing on the green.

Blake glanced at Kaz now and then, amazed as ever at how well the younger man coped. But, then, this was just craggy moorland and the guy had, against all odds, scaled the 8,848 meters to the peak of Mount Everest. He admired his friend's courage immensely, doubted that he would cope so well himself given the same circumstances.

"There's Fenfeld," Blake said, as the small village at last came into view, nestled in the rocky landscape below them. "In about half an hour, we'll be sitting in the pub enjoying a pint."

"Let's sit here for a bit, watch the sun set," Kaz suggested, as Sol began to touch the horizon and the firmament was tinted with crimson and flame amber.

"Good idea," he agreed, with a nod. "It's a fantastic view."

They took off their backpacks. Blake got out the picnic rug for them to sit on. Kaz got out the flask of coffee and poured the last of it into two enamel mugs, passing one to his companion.

"Thanks." Blake smiled and took a mouthful of the strong, now lukewarm beverage.

They could hear a dog barking in the distance, and then the peal of church bells also drifted to their ears. The sky was now a nacreous mix, and somewhere an early owl hooted, as our closest star sank lower and twilight encroached.

Blake shifted awkwardly, put his jacket across his lap to hide the fact that his cock was straining in its fabric prison.

"What have you been thinking about, sitting there? Certainly not just the view!" Kaz said and proffered a knowing smile.

Fuck! His discretion had been in vain. Kaz was too

keenly observant, had obviously recognized the subtle signs. Blake didn't reply, merely shrugged and avoided eye contact, but Kaz didn't let it go.

"You're horny," he stated bluntly. He bit his lip and looked coy. "You know, if you really want to blow a wad... I mean, it wouldn't be the first time, would it? We did it at Simon and Christine's wedding. No strings, just a fuck-buddy thing. We could use that old shepherd's hut we saw. What d'you say?"

Blake looked at him then, gave an awkward half-smile. They'd never really talked about what had happened between them at their friend's wedding. It had been a lovely ceremony. Christine, wearing a stunning, Victorian-style ivory gown, had arrived at the small country church in a horse-drawn carriage. The church had been filled with an abundance of white and lilac flowers. A peal of six bells had rung out for twenty minutes before the wedding, and for about fifteen minutes after, in glorious auditory celebration.

Kaz had noticed his friend's absence during the photo session and had gone in search of him. He'd discovered the suntanned hunk jacking off in a small, ancient mausoleum in the older, semi-wild part of the graveyard. Crimson-cheeked with embarrassment, Blake had quickly zipped up his flies but the Kaz had, without a word, dropped his pants and leaned forward against the cold stone wall. It was an invitation Blake couldn't turn down. He swiftly retrieved the just-in-case condom he kept in his wallet and there ensued a brief, rough fucking. It was thrilling! The spontaneity, the risk of being caught, the feeling of decadent wickedness...

Blake closed his eyes and sighed, heavily. He could still hear that dog barking and the church bells ringing out. His cock throbbed, pressed uncomfortably against his zipper. Damn, he wanted Kaz, so much, right now! But was it wise? If they screwed for a second time, would Kaz expect it to lead to a regular fuck-buddy relationship? He wasn't up for that, simply, because it would mean he'd have to reveal his fetish to Kaz.

Fetish. He didn't like that word. It evoked images of leather, whips and chains, guys obsessing over feet, or dressing up as babies. Not that there was anything wrong with that sort of thing: whatever rocks your boat, as they say. But, to him, the word just didn't seem appropriate for his own personal desire. He wasn't into pain, dressing up, role play, or screwing teddy bears. Just like everyone, he liked to fuck, but only under certain circumstances. It was a fetish, by definition, though—*'something whose presence is psychologically necessary for sexual gratification'*.

"Blake? Earth to Blake!" Kaz nudged his shoulder, jolting him from his reverie. With a cheeky grin, he grabbed his groin and squeezed. "You don't want to waste a good boner when there's a hungry hole, ready and waiting."

Blake was so turned on now, and his companion so eager, biology bested brains and he caved in to his androgen-fueled urges.

"The hut was some way back. I'm going to do you right here," he told him, already unzipping his flies, allowing his aching member to spring free. Why not? There was no one around: it was way more private than the graveyard had been. It was a warm enough evening, and alfresco sex was always so exhilarating.

Kaz didn't object to the location. With bright eyes and a captivating smile, the younger man stripped down to just his shirt. He also removed his prosthesis. Blake watched him with hungry eyes. God, how he fancied that lithe, athletic body! The younger man's disability certainly didn't prevent him from keeping fit. Proffering a return smile, he removed his walking boots, then his trousers and briefs. Making sure that the picnic rug was within easy reach to cover them if some dog walker or hiker should appear, he lay on his side next to Kaz. Then Blake did something he certainly hadn't done in the graveyard. He leaned in and kissed him full on the lips, probed his tongue into his mouth. He tasted of spearmint.

Kaz moaned into the kiss. He pressed his body close to Blake's and their hard erections rubbed against one another. Blake reached an arm around the other's sinewy body and caressed a taut buttock. When the kiss broke, he moved his mouth lower, suckling softly at Kaz's neck, then showering his hard chest with quick light kisses. He ran his tongue down his torso to his navel, paused to lick the belly-pucker before moving still lower and sucking on his pulsing helmet. Kaz groaned and dribbled pre-cum into his lover's mouth. Blake then pulled away and rolled onto his back.

"Haven't got any lube," he said huskily.

"Spit's good enough," Kaz replied, his timbre soft and low. "If you're going to cloak the captain, I've an ultra-lube condom in my jacket pocket."

Blake retrieved the condom and put it on. Then he spat on his finger and rubbed it against Kaz's tight rear hole. He eased the digit in and fingered his friend for a few moments, making him groan and arch his hips. Then he firmly planted his palms on the ground, either side of the other man's shoulders, and smiled down at him, pressing his rock hard cock against his belly.

"You look as sexy as hell," he told him, holding his gaze for a long moment. He dipped his head to kiss him again before pushing himself up onto his knees. He shoved his hands beneath the younger man's buttocks and lifted him up, then pressed the head of his cock against his puckered hole. Kaz raised his leg and rested it on his lover's right shoulder. Blake eased himself in, moaning in pleasure as the warm tightness sucked him inside, engulfing his throbbing rod. He remained still for a minute, allowing Kaz to adjust to the sensation of him inside his ass, before he began to ride him with long smooth strokes.

"You've got such a pretty prick," Blake commented, watching Kaz's smooth, vein-less cock bouncing up and down on his washboard belly as he rocked to and fro with Blake's rhythmic thrusts. Kaz gave a throaty laugh. Blake shifted his weight slightly so he could free one hand. He firmly grasped the small but beautiful cock and squeezed and stroked, causing Kaz to moan even louder. Groaning, grunting, gargled exclamations, the slap of balls on flesh, intermingled with gently rustling leaves and the sustained churring trill of a male night-jar.

"I'm going to come!" Blake announced, before spewing out the warm sticky fluid into the silicon reservoir.

Kaz was beyond articulation. Eyes wide, chest heaving, back arched, he opened his mouth wide in a silent, orgasmic scream as he spurted semen over his belly and chest. *An ethereal carnal vision*, Blake thought, as he looked down at him for a few moments, panting softly, before slowly pulling out and removing the condom. He wrapped it in a paper tissue from his pants pocket before flopping down beside Kaz on soft, asparagus-colored moss. He got his breath back before giving his friend a quick peck on the lips then standing up and dressing. Kaz put his prosthetic above-the-knee left leg back on, and then got dressed.

The night air was still, and almost silent now, as they made their way down the last slope to the village. The bells had ceased, the dog was no longer barking, the night-jar had flown away and the sleepy country settlement was quieter than the graveyard had been the first time they'd had sex. The two men reached the pub tired out, from both their long hike and their carnal activities. They booked into the twin room they'd reserved then showered together before going back downstairs for a pub meal and a couple of pints of cider to wash it down. An early night was certainly on the cards and neither had any trouble at all falling asleep about an hour later.

***

"You got laid!" Rayne declared, handing Kaz a glass of white wine and flopping down on the couch next to him.

"Rayne! That's none of your business," he replied, blushing slightly but suppressing a grin, all the same. He leaned forward to take a slice of the large take-out pizza from the box and ate a mouthful before asking, "How the fuck can you tell, anyway?"

"Your aura's different when you've got laid," the thirty-something redhead replied. "You know how they say you can tell when a woman's pregnant because she's blooming? Well, when you've had sex, you're kinda blooming."

"What rubbish!" Kaz laughed, shaking his head.

"Who was it?"

"Oh no, don't go there. I'm not telling."

"Was it Blake again?"

Kaz almost choked on his mouthful of pizza. He swallowed, coughed, frowned.

"What do you mean, '*again*'?"

"You did it at Simon and Christine's wedding," she stated in a matter-of-fact voice. She took a sip of her wine before continuing. "You surely didn't think we hadn't noticed? Blake slipped away, you followed then, about twenty minutes later, you reappeared together. And you were most definitely blooming. So what's with you two? Is it serious or just a friends-with-benefits thing?"

Kaz sighed and shrugged, took a gulp of wine before answering.

"To be honest, I really don't know," he told her. "There's always been a chemistry, right from the first moment we met, but we've not acted on it, never spoken about it. It's been like a silent agreement to ignore it. At first I thought it was because of this..." He patted his left thigh. He was wearing his more realistic prosthesis, the one he kept for everyday use, rather than the more versatile, lightweight, custom-made one he used for hiking, climbing and sports. "Then, as I got to know him better, I realized that was a horrible misjudgment. Anyway, time went by and I thought I'd slipped securely into the friend zone. Until the wedding... We've only done it the twice and both times I initiated it. The first time was a quick shag - a wham, bam, thank you man thing. But yesterday—wow. This time, it was way more intimate. There was foreplay, we kissed... I dunno. Like I said, there's a chemistry. I really like him and I think he feels the same. Something's holding him back, though, and I don't know what."

"You should talk to him, tell him how you feel, and see what he says," Rayne advised. She glanced at her watch. "Why not go see him, right now? No time like the present, as they say: no procrastinating."

"Sunday evening—incommunicado time, remember,"

he laughed. "Alone time to disconnect, unwind, reboot his brain."

Blake had always insisted on spending Sunday evenings alone. Some of the guys had thought perhaps he went to church, to the Evensong service, but Kaz knew from conversation that his friend, whilst very spiritual, was definitely not a church-goer. "Everyone needs some time out," Kaz had commented at the time. "Nothing mysterious or secretive about it. He probably meditates or just watches movies with a few cans."

***

Blake looked forward to Sunday evenings. He always followed the same routine. First he lit two candles, one on each of the nightstands, then a sandalwood-scented incense stick; his favorite aroma. He fetched a clean cotton bath sheet and laid it out on the bed. Finally he opened the window a few inches before stripping off and lying down on the bed. The preparation was finished and, now, all he had to do was wait a few moments.

About five minutes later, the church bells rang out, summoning worshippers to evening prayer. The melodious sound of the six cast bronze bells sang to Blake in an evocative, emotive peal. He lay there, with his arms folded behind his head, a soft contented smile on his ruggedly handsome face, listening to the heavenly music. Soon his thick, heavily-veined cock began to twitch, then to grow and harden, until it was engorged and throbbing. Blake reached out for a bottle of baby oil from the nightstand, poured some onto his palm, and massaged it over his rock hard length. He began to slowly slide his hand up and down his shaft, moaning softly. He closed his eyes, took slow deep breaths, silently told himself not to rush this ethereal pleasure, but to make it last as long as possible.

As Blake increased the speed and pressure, his breathing quickened and he moaned more loudly. With each downward stroke, his hand pressed into his tightening balls. He raised his ass up off the bed slightly, groaned, moved his hand faster still. Twice he squeezed his purplish helmet, hard, to delay his orgasm. He couldn't hold back for very long, though. Just as the last, lingering notes drifted away and the bells fell into silence, the man grunted loudly, arched his back, and spewed out a stream of translucent, white-tinted spunk that landed on his belly and broad, hirsute chest.

***

Kaz was munching on a slice of toast with lime marmalade, and pondering. A notion had suddenly come to mind as he lay awake, unable to sleep, in the early hours. He just couldn't shake the thought from his head. It was absurd, incongruous and yet, somehow, it did make sense. He couldn't possibly broach the subject with Blake, though, surely? If he did, the other would probably laugh his head off and call him crazy. It wasn't something he was likely to admit to, even in the unlikely event it was true, anyhow. He should just dismiss the matter, and yet he couldn't. There were streams of thought meandering through his mind and feeding into a lake of suspicion.

The young man suddenly realized that there was one sure way to disprove his hypothesis. He simply had to get hold of a copy of the local parish magazine. One came through the letterbox each month but, being an atheist himself, he always put it straight in the paper recycling crate without reading it. So now he abandoned his half-eaten toast and went rummaging through the junk mail, take-out menus, and used envelopes to recover the latest copy of the church booklet. He retrieved it and sat down to flick through the pages.

A letter from the vicar. An appeal for toys for the church nursery. Adverts for local tradesmen. Announcements of baptisms, weddings and funerals. Obituaries. Days and times of services. And what Kaz was seeking—the day and time of bell-ringing practice.

Damn! So that backfired. He'd hoped the magazine would instantly dispel his hunch but instead it actually added more weight to the albeit circumstantial evidence. He frowned, chewing on his lower lip, as he contemplated what to do—if anything. If he was content to remain merely friends then the answer would be to do nothing; to mind his own business. But was he content to be just friends? Did he want to explore the possibility of being so much more?

***

Kaz was too aware of his heart beating: his stomach felt

hollow, and his palms were sweating. Could he actually go through with this? What if he lost Blake's friendship? He couldn't bear the thought.

Blake opened the dark green front door and waved to his unexpected visitor. He had obviously heard the car pulling into his driveway. Well, there was no turning back now.

"Hi! What brings you here?" Blake asked, in a cheerful voice, as Kaz walked up the cobbled path to the former rectory. Built by the Church of England around 1900 and close to St. Mary's, the parish church of Castorvale, the redbrick house was pretty and welcoming.

"Sorry for the surprise visit, but I wanted to talk about something," he replied.

"You don't have to apologize, stupid. You're my best buddy, you're welcome any time," Blake told him, opening the door wider so his friend could enter. "Cup of tea, or a bottle of beer?"

"Beer, thanks," Kaz replied. Hopefully alcohol would provide the courage he needed to actually go through with this.

Blake grabbed two cans of beer from the fridge, passed one to Kaz, then flopped down in an armchair.

"So, what do you want to talk about? Not still nervous about that job interview? You've got a great resume, plenty of experience, excellent references—you'll do great."

"Actually... Um... Well, I got you this." He passed Blake a small gift-wrapped present. Blake raised an eyebrow.

"What's the occasion?" he queried. "It's not my birthday for another month." Kaz just shrugged his shoulders, gave a shy half-smile. Blake tore off the plain blue paper to reveal a CD.

"Carillon Bells!" he exclaimed in surprise.

"Yeah. I've no idea what carillon is, but it's got a picture of bells on the front so I guessed you'd like it."

"It's a musical instrument, with cast bronze, cup-shaped bells that play melodies," his friend explained. "The first was in Flanders in 1510. The largest in the world has seventy-seven bells. It's in Daejeon, South Korea. I'd love to go and hear it one day."

"You know a lot about them."

"A nerdy interest. I did a project on them back in college, eons ago. I really appreciate this, thanks. I can't imagine how you knew I'd like it though."

"Lucky hunch," Kaz replied. "So, why don't you put it on?" He suspected Blake would find some excuse not to.

"I'm going to wait until a bit later on in the evening," Blake told him. "I love listening to music, with a glass of wine by a nice log fire, for a while before bed. It's relaxing."

Knew it! Relaxing, my ass!

"But I'd love to know what it sounds like," Kaz persisted.

"Actually, I was just about to watch a TV program before you arrived."

"So record it. Or watch it on catch-up later," Kaz suggested. "Why do you like bells so much?"

"They're so powerful. Bells have the ability to amaze, enthrall, charm, frighten, warn, can raise your spirits so high or instill a terrible dread," Blake replied, speaking with such intense emotion. "In mysticism, they say the flat circular bottom represents the horizon of the earth, the empty space within symbolizes all that exists between heaven and earth, and the clapper is the tongue, the voice of divinity. That voice speaks to me, in a way. And, yes, I know I sound crazy."

"I don't think you sound crazy, just passionate about your interest. Nothing wrong in that."

"Well, no more passionate crazy talk, I promise," Blake laughed. He glanced at his watch. "Fancy a walk down to the pub?"

"No, I don't," Kaz replied flatly. He gave a coy smile. "I'd much rather we grab another beer, head upstairs to the bedroom. We can put that CD on, so you can get all horny and give me a good rumble between the sheets."

Blake spluttered out his mouthful of beer and stared at his friend. He looked gobsmacked. His didn't say a word, just sat there, agape. Silent moments passed. Kaz fidgeted, awkwardly.

"Both times we've had sex, there were bells ringing..." Kaz was the first to speak. He didn't get to finish his sentence.

"Coincidence," Blake interjected.

"I'd have thought so, too, if it wasn't for the other stuff."

"What other stuff?" Blake demanded, his tone and body language defensive.

"You want me to go over it all? Like, how you avoid going out on Wednesdays, which just happens to be the night there's bell practice at the church? Or how, at New Year, as soon as those bells start ringing, you disappear for about twenty minutes? Every year. I'd bet a week's wages you were jacking off. Shall I go on or are you just going to admit it? You don't need to freak out about my knowing. We all have our kinks and fetishes."

"And we keep them to ourselves."

"Except from our closest friend. That one person you can always trust. The one person you know will never laugh, or judge, or tell. The one person in the world you can always confide in."

Blake raked both hands through his hair and sighed. Then, to Kaz's great relief, the man smiled.

"Okay, okay. You don't have to guilt-trip me into confessing. Yeah, you're my best mate, and I know I can always tell you anything. So... Sure, yes, I get turned on by bells. I'm a bell fetishist. It's something I thought I was hiding pretty well."

"I like aprons," Kaz suddenly announced.

"Huh?"

"Aprons. Frilly ones. The sort worn by maids, and waitresses, and 1950s housewives. I love them. I have this fantasy where I'm wearing nothing but a frilly white apron and... Well, you get the idea. It's a kink rather than a fetish. I don't actually need an apron to get horny but, if one can be utilized for sex occasionally, then all the better." He grinned at Blake. "You're allowed to laugh. Imagine the sight of me wearing nothing but a white frilly apron and a boner!"

That revelation certainly lightened the mood. Both men started to laugh and soon they were laughing so much that tears were streaming down their faces, and Kaz had a stitch.

"Explains why you decided to leave town and live way out here in the sticks," Kaz commented as the hilarity calmed. "A rectory's the perfect place for you."

"I know. I couldn't believe my luck when this place came up for sale."

"Fancy that walk down to the pub now?"

"No. I fancy your suggestion. Beer, bells, and tangled bed sheets."

***

An avian evensong echoed stridently from the green canopy, and the cool breeze carried with it the spicy fragrance of the night-flowering Gladiolus Tristis. Blake drew in a deep breath, savoring the farrago of scents and sounds, before going indoors. As he locked the front door, threw his keys down on the sideboard, and headed for the stairs, he could hear Kaz in the kitchen. Blake smiled to himself as he went up to the bedroom. He partly opened the window, lit two candles, one on each of the nightstands, and a sandalwood incense stick. He took a tube of anal lubricant from a drawer and put it within easy reach on the nightstand. Blake took a quick shower, the aroma of ginger and black pepper shower gel assailing his senses as he lathered his torso and washed his hair. After that, he lay on the bed, eyes closed, totally relaxed, waiting for the blissfully erotic, sonorous ringing of church bells. He had always loved Wednesday evenings, almost as much as Sundays, but they were even more wonderful now he had at last shared his secret fetish with Kaz. He no longer had to jack off alone when the bells got him horny, not with his lover offering a pretty pucker eager to be plunged.

A rich cascade of sound dominated the airwaves as the six bells, from treble to tenor, rang out. Blake's attuned ear could detect the hums sharp of true-harmonic and primes flat of true-harmonic, a trait typical of old-style, English bells. As the team of bell-ringers pulled on the ropes, swinging the bells to and fro, Blake pulled on his cock, stroking and stretching, moaning softly. Once he was rock hard and throbbing, he slathered on some of the thick anal lube then got up from the bed and slipped downstairs, his bare feet near-silent on the deep pile carpet.

For a moment, he stood silently in the doorway, watching his near-nude lover busying about in the old-fashioned country kitchen. The window was slightly ajar. The coffee machine was wafting an evocative Arabica aroma. Kaz was wearing nothing but a white cotton pinafore apron, trimmed with lace. Blake's cock throbbed, achingly, as he listened to the resonant peal and thought about fucking that cute taut ass.

Blake felt Kaz start a little as he crept up behind him and wrapped his muscular arms around him. The younger man then laughed lightly, pressed back against his lover.

"I didn't hear you come in the room."

"I was very quiet. I wanted to just watch you for a while. But now I have to touch you, convince myself you're really here and not merely a vision."

"You don't have to be silver-tongued to get up my bum, you know," Kaz told him with a cheeky chuckle.

Blake nibbled at his ear lobe then kissed his neck. One hand wandered to the smooth semi-erection beneath the apron, stroked his length and fondled his balls, whilst the other hand went to play with a taut nipple. Kaz moaned beneath the sensual touch and leaned forward, bracing himself against the scrubbed pine table. Blake's hands moved to Kaz's hips as he went down onto his knees behind his lover and buried his face in the crack between the firm butt cheeks. His tongue slavered, and probed at the rosebud entrance and Kaz groaned, thrust back his hips, gripped more tightly to the table's edge.

"Aaah. That feels so good," Kaz murmured. "Don't make me wait, though. Fuck me, right now. Please."

Blake certainly wasn't going to refuse. He stood back up, wrapped one strong arm around Kaz's torso, and guided the tip of his helmet to the man's hungry hole. Kaz gasped as his lover struggled against the resistance of the sphincter muscle, briefly then plunged in to the hilt. He stayed still until Kaz pushed his hips back slightly and took that as the signal to start thrusting. He shoved in and out with a steady rhythm, grunting and groaning, his face contorting with strains of pleasure. Every muscle taut, warm skin flushed pink, intermingled limbs; no defining line where one body ended and another began; sinewy torsos entwined, vinelike, with one another in euphoric coupling.

"I'm... I'm gonna come," Blake warned him, as heat pooled and muscles contracted. He let out a raw, guttural sound as he spurted his large, sticky load into his lover, condoms having been abandoned after a frank discussion. He didn't pull out at once, but remained buried inside the warm haven until he felt Kaz's own orgasm kick in, felt the man's stickiness spill out over his hand. Then he showered the back of his neck and shoulders with small kisses as he eased out of him.

Blake turned Kaz around and kissed him passionately, tongues dancing an erotic tango, hands tangling into hair. When the kiss broke, Blake removed Kaz's apron, letting it fall to the floor, and swept the man up in his arms. He carried him upstairs and laid him on the bed. He removed the younger man's prosthesis himself, setting it down carefully, and pulled the covers over them both.

"It's too early to go to sleep," Kaz told him. Blake smiled.

"Who said anything about sleep?" he replied, running

a hand down his thigh. "Bell practice goes on for two hours. My dong can ding you a few more times, tonight."

About the Author

A writer of mostly gay erotic fiction but also some other genres, also an historian, pagan, father, teacher and resident of planet earth. After an active and unusual life travelling the globe, living in a round hut, tackling white water rapids, and sleeping in 5000 year old rock tombs, I now live a peaceful semi-retired family life in the North with my youngest son and my adult daughter.

SOFT
by Sonni de Soto

GRETA LOCKETT STEPPED UP to the line, behind a fresh-faced freshman girl, waiting in front of the Haut Cafe counter. She took a deep breath, the scent of freshly brewing coffee wafting to her and making her smile.

God, she loved their coffee.

And their pastries.

And Bryan Harlow, the long-haired guy behind the counter.

He gave a lopsided, lazy grin to the girl while he handed her a cup of coffee. Bryan was cute in an *aw-shucks,* shy kind of way. The kind of boy first crushes were made for. She was sure he'd had his name scrawled on notebook covers and textbook margins in longing scrawl and wishful hearts. His big, deep, brown eyes were fringed by long, full lashes, and his almost too full lips always looked soft and just a little slick from his near-constant licking.

She watched him take crumpled dollars and random coins from the redheaded underclassman.

They looked cute together. A cute couple. Petite and pigtailed, the redhead was the girl-next-door all grown up. Greta watched Bryan take the money from the girl's hand and wondered what it would look like if his hand clasped hers. If her small, slim hand cupped his cheek. If his earthy hands moved over her celestial body, circling the whole of her tiny form in the orbit of his arms. With room to spare.

She fit him.

In a way that Greta couldn't even imagine doing.

Bryan looked up from the change he was about to put into the register and spotted Greta in line. His lopsided smile widened. "I'll be done in a minute; I just need to finish this sale and grab my stuff."

Greta just nodded, her throat feeling tight, when the girl turned to see who he was talking to. Greta saw her eyes widen, then narrow as she studied Greta in confusion.

She knew what she saw.

Greta was a big girl.

She'd always been a big girl. Not just tall, though at 5' 10" she was that. She was *big*. *Big-boned,* her mother called her. *Plus-sized,* her size-12 baby sister insisted. *Fat* was what she heard them say whenever they did. At a size 24, Greta was only too aware of what she was.

And, though she styled her shiny, healthy, blond hair well, applied her makeup perfectly, and always wore colorful, stylish clothes that flattered her, she knew that none of that changed what she was. It helped—don't get her wrong; she'd long since accepted that she was big and that didn't mean she couldn't also be beautiful—but she was what she was.

And she was all too well aware that, when paired next to Bryan, she and he didn't make sense. No matter how many times or how closely, how sweetly, he held her, she knew that there was nothing she could do to change that.

She watched Bryan untie his apron from hips that were significantly smaller than her own. When he headed back into the kitchen to grab his things, the girl turned around to face her.

A part of Greta wanted to meet the girl's gaze, to look straight into her eyes and tell her that, yes, the cute baker boy was dating the fat chick, like some bad and impossible cliché.

And she would have. Probably. If, even after nine months, it'd made any sense to her, either. But there was—would likely always be—that part of her that stared at that girl next to her and wondered what Bryan was thinking. Wondered why, of all the girls he could have, he chose to be with her.

***

Bryan stared at Greta leaning against the head of his bed, her legs spread out on his duvet. "God, you're gorgeous."

She rolled her eyes dismissively. "Thank you."

She clearly didn't get it, and he didn't understand how she couldn't see it. She was all sweeping curves and sassy sway, she was exactly the type of woman he went for. She was the definition of *full-figured*. When he held her, he *held* her. She filled his embrace. When he squeezed her, her body, like her heart, was giving and warm. With his arms wrapped around her, he felt grounded and grateful.

And, God knew, girl had an ass and a rack that made his mouth water and his heart race.

But, beyond that, she was smart and funny and adventurous. He loved how eager she always was to try new things.

He'd never known anyone with the same kind of appetites as him. For food. For excitement. For sex. Too often, with other girls he'd been with, he'd been accused of being insatiable. Greedy. Gluttonous. The girls he'd known had been so easily sated. Had played safe. Had stopped short. Had always seemed a little afraid of reaching their fill.

But Greta was the kind of girl who always gave as good as she got. She shared and fueled his hungers. She was the kind of girl with whom enough didn't have to be enough. With her, he didn't have to settle. Never had to go still hungry for more. With her, he still felt gluttonous and decadent but, instead of shame or denial, he could only feel joy and anticipation.

He'd been doing kink for nine months now with Greta. Nothing too wild, mostly dealing with denial and edging play, where she teased him mercilessly before finally allowing him release. They'd played and explored enough to have a good grasp on what each other enjoyed. What places to touch. What tools to use. How long to linger.

Thrilled with the kinks Greta had introduced him to, he couldn't help but wonder whether some of the fantasies he'd thought were just nonsensical fap-fodder could be more.

He bit his lip and paced a bit beside his bed. "Do you," he asked, lifting his shoulder in an awkward shrug, "have any kinks that you haven't told me—told anyone—about?"

She turned to tuck one leg underneath her and faced him. "Not since I started exploring my kinks." Her gaze narrowed. "Do you?"

Bryan felt his face flush under her gaze. "Well." God, why was this so hard? He shrugged and licked his lips. He swallowed dryly. "I do have one." He took a fortifying breath. "I just don't know if you'll be into it. I don't want to..." His voice trailed off. Frowning, he stared at the fullness of her, imagining as he tried to find the words. Upset her? Hurt her with it? "Offend you."

She let out a huff and rolled her eyes at him. "I already know that you're into fat chicks."

He snapped straight. "What?"

She gave him an indulgent look. "You like BBWs. *Big, beautiful women.*" She gestured to herself. "I kinda figured that out on my own."

Bryan frowned and his spine stiffened. "You're not fat." Big? Maybe. Beautiful? Definitely. But *fat*? It was just such a harsh-sounding word for a woman like her. Like an insult for something he found inspiring. "You're soft."

She snorted. "And, by *soft*, you mean *fat*." She gave him another placating look. "It's okay to say it."

"No." He walked toward her, each step deliberate with demand. He wanted her to understand. "I mean *soft*," he said, taking her hand to pull her up against him, "as in the opposite of me." With a hand on her hip, he held her close, so the lovely, warm give of her middle pressed flush against every inch of his hard length.

He felt her breath hitch, a shiver that echoed all over her body in an arousing jiggle. He looked down as awareness flared in her eyes. Instinctively, his eyes dropped to her breasts, lush and supple, that rose and fell with each shallow, aroused breath. He felt a smile spread across his face. "Do you trust me?"

"To do what?"

He held her close. "To show you."

***

Greta sat on the edge of Bryan's bed. He'd told her to wait while he got things ready.

Ready for what, she had no idea. He wouldn't tell her. He wanted to show her.

"It won't hurt," he'd promised her. "And we can stop whenever you want."

So she'd agreed. Why not? She knew Bryan. He was such a gentle person; she didn't think there was anything he could do to really scare her.

Not like that, anyway.

If she was honest, she'd been worried earlier. She

wasn't even sure she could say what she'd been worried about.

That he was breaking up with her? Sure, it was always a worry in the back of her head. Even though she hated to admit it, part of her was constantly waiting for Bryan to leave her.

That he wasn't actually into the things, the kinks, that they'd tried? Oh, absolutely. She'd been with enough guys who'd looked at her desires—at her—and run. She'd had friends—and even some family members - find out her secrets and shame her for them. Bryan always seemed eager, and more than interested in their games, but Greta couldn't help but worry that it was just too good to be true.

But her biggest worry had begun to stir within her while she'd watched him squirm in front of her. She worried that he *was* into her and *was* into everything they were doing, but not in the way she wanted. That, after being with a girl like her, he was overthinking and overanalyzing it. Turning it into its own fetish.

Which, maybe it was.

But she'd known men with fat-girl fetishes. Men who saw her weight and nothing else. Men who took one look at her and thought they knew her. Who thought fat girls were desperate or lonely. Who thought she ought to be grateful for any attention they threw her way. Or that she should be willing to do anything they asked, just to keep them. Those men saw her bigger form and assumed that she was less than a person.

Bryan wasn't like that. She knew that. Bryan might

love her curves, but he also loved her. The whole of her.

But those men had left scars on her psyche that she'd have for the rest of her life, and it was hard not to feel them some days.

"Are you ready?"

She looked up at Bryan when he peeked back into the room.

She could see excitement in his eyes, tempered with nerves.

Was she ready?

She rubbed her hands on her thighs—just to stall—before standing up and following him out into the hallway.

He led her to the kitchen. He pulled out a chair for her. But, when she moved to sit in it, he stopped her. He held out a hand to help her climb up on the chair.

She gave him a bemused look, but took his hand and stepped up onto the chair. Sitting on the edge of the table, she tucked her ankles underneath her and rested her feet on the chair. "Okay." She shrugged, a slight smile teasing her lips. "What now?"

"Well." He turned toward the countertops. "It's something that I've thought of before." He shook his head. "Of course, I have. It's not really original or anything. And it feels really dumb." He turned back around with a piping bag in hand. "But I just really like it."

Her gaze narrowed on the brightly colored frosting in the tipped bag. He wanted to frost her? Really? That sounded...

Messy.

She looked down at her clothes. Well, these had to go. She loved this outfit—every piece of it, from sweater to shapewear—and she liked it much better without frosting all over it.

Except...

Even though they'd been together nine months, she'd never been *that* naked in front of him. She liked to undress in the dark or under flattering, dim mood lighting. Most of the time, she liked to keep something on, her shirt, or dress, or even a nice bodice or corset. Especially during sex, when the sound and feel of her flesh jiggling or slapping made her feel anything but sexy.

Her clothes were her armor, particularly in those moments. They showcased and enhanced the parts of herself the she was proud of and hid the parts she'd rather conceal.

Without them...

She looked at him and bit her lip.

It was asking a lot, and she wasn't even sure if he realized that.

Bryan's lips faltered into a frown. "You're not into this." He winced and let his arms drop. "This was a dumb idea, wasn't it?" He shook his head. "I'm sorry. I just thought..." He huffed. "I'm sorry."

"No." Greta swallowed hard. No. "It's not dumb." If it

was what he wanted, it wasn't dumb. "I just..." She could do this. For him. She took a good look at him, as well as a deep breath, before shifting to sit more fully on the table. "I have rules."

Bryan tilted his head in surprise before nodding. "Okay, what are they?"

She bit her lip. "One," she said, ticking off on her fingers, "no frosting near my naughty bits." She gestured to her lap. With all that bacteria-feeding sugar, that was just a bad infection waiting to happen.

Bryan smiled. "Okay." He nodded.

"Two," she said, flicking out another finger, "I want to watch." She didn't understand this, but she wanted to.

"Um, sure." He winced a little. "But no judgments; I'm not as good as I want to be."

"Of course." Who was she to judge, anyway? "And, lastly, clothes come off only as needed, okay?"

His brow furrowed. "You want to keep your clothes on?" He looked confused. "For this?"

As much as possible, yes. She squirmed a bit. "If that's okay." She wanted to be into this. She wanted this to be sexy and playful. But it was hard to get in the mood for playful, sexy times with all these nerves and self-conscious anxieties inside her.

Bryan shrugged. "Okay, I accept all that." He looked at her daringly. "But, to get started, your pants need to come off."

Greta looked down and wiggled her legs and toes.

Yeah, that was true.

She reached beneath her sweater to undo her jeans. She shoved them down, reminding herself that she'd done this with him—undressed in front of him—countless times before. That, despite the bright lights and avid attention, this was no different.

But it was different.

Which seemed silly. It was just frosting.

Powdered sugar, butter, and some food dye.

It wasn't even that kinky, not since that nineties' teen movie with the whipped cream bikini.

This wasn't a big deal.

Except it was.

Usually, when they had sex or played, she liked to be in control. Not necessarily as a top or a Domme, per se, she just found it beneficial to direct his attention toward some things and away from other things. If he tried to undress her, she'd undress him first. If his hands strayed too close to parts of herself she wasn't quite comfortable with, like her tummy, her hips, her thighs, then she'd reach for him. Like some sexual sleight of hand, she'd become an expert at refocusing their sex on him and his body.

But this was different.

She stared at the piping bags with their metal tips, looking harsh and judgmental. To do this, he needed to be up close and focused on her body.

She wrinkled her nose. She could do this. For him, she could.

So, she sat still, while he leaned in close over her legs,

piping bag in hand. When she felt the icing touch her skin, she sucked in a deep breath and tensed. And, despite her saying she wanted to watch, she shut her eyes.

She could feel the sugar and grease, squeezed from the bag, oozing onto her. She felt it coat her as he drew lines and swirls and dots over the bones of her feet. She swore she could feel it seep, sticky and sharply sweet, like a cavity on her nerves.

"Remember when you told me about that one guy?" she heard Bryan's voice say softly. "The one obsessed with your feet?"

She blinked, thinking back. Lenny Wilson. "Sure." She smiled a little at the memory. "He bought most of the shoes I own." Lenny had been the kind of guy who'd loved her despite her weight. He'd been so taken by her feet; by her high arches and well-turned toes, and even the swell of her ankles, that he could overlook the rest of the package. And, for a while, she'd enjoyed the attention, like shoes and massages, he'd lavished on them. That was back when *plus-size fashion* had seemed like an oxymoron, and shoes were the one clothing item that fit well and looked pretty. He'd always said that it didn't matter what your waist-size was, anyone can fit into a sexy shoe.

She'd smack any man who said something like that to her, now. But back then... "He was the first guy to make me feel like there was something beautiful about me. Even if it was just my feet."

"Well, you do have nice feet." Bryan added flourishes

here and there on her toes. "Soft and well-shaped. I get why someone would want to worship them." Then she felt him begin to frost up her ankle and calves. "But, look at you; there are a lot of beautiful things about you."

"Thank you." Greta gave him a small smile. It was a corny line. Obligatory boyfriend banter.

"I mean it; you're gorgeous, Greta." He sighed. "I wish you could see it."

She opened her eyes to reflexively thank him again, when she saw the design he'd made on her feet.

Green vines with blooming leaves and delicate violet, red, and blue flowers twined over her skin. She watched his hands draw vines that climbed up, toward her knee, with swift, sure flicks of his capable hands.

She wiggled her little toe, just a bit, feeling the icing harden there. It tickled, and made her want to scratch or shake it. But the tiny flower, nestled there at the crook of her toe, was so fragile and pretty it felt wrong to disturb it.

So she sat very still, fighting against the violent need to move vibrating in her limbs. She felt that sensation, that urge, that need, channel itself within her, cycling through her like an electric current. Suddenly, she could feel the weight of each line of frosting. She felt the curl in every tiny sugared petal. Like seeds beneath her skin, she could almost feel the possibilities of where his garden would grow on her flesh.

She blinked, amazed. "It's beautiful."

***

"Thanks." He grinned, glad she liked it. He looked back at the design he'd done on her legs, quite proud of himself.

"Okay." He wiped his hands on the towel he'd tucked into his waistband. "Want to do the rest of you?"

Bryan stood back and watched her lift her heavy sweater over her head, revealing some kind of black, sleek, zip-up undergarment that made both his mouth salivate and his hands want to tear it off.

"What about that?" He gestured to the garment.

She raised her eyebrow. "Do you need me to take my shapewear off?" A protective hand rested over her middle, making him frown.

He didn't *need* it. But he really, really, really wanted it.

Greta had lots of sexy underwear. More so than any other girl he'd ever known. And, while part of him appreciated it—she did look amazing in it—a part of him hated it.

Hidden beneath all the zippers and hooks and cloth were parts of Greta she never let anyone else see. Not even him.

And he wanted to see.

But, even in their most intimate moments, she kept them on. Kept her defenses and her guard up.

And it wasn't that he wanted to take them from her; he never wanted to *take* anything from her, but he wished he could let her know it was okay to let them down herself. To let him in.

She took an audibly deep breath. "Okay." She reached for the black piece's front clasp, but her fingers lingered hesitantly. "But, first, can I ask why?"

"Why?" Why he needed her to take off her clothes?

Because he wanted her naked? Wasn't that reason enough?

She shrugged. "I know it's a little silly to ask people why they're into what they're into. Most of the time the answer is just *because I am*." She shrugged again. "But why frosting?"

Oh.

That.

He took a deep breath. How to explain it.

He shrugged and shifted his feet a bit. "It's not really about the frosting." He scrunched his face and looked up at the ceiling, trying to find his words. "It's more about having you, this stunning and amazing woman, laid out in front of me." Like a blank canvas or moldable clay.

He wished he could paint or sculpt her. Hell, he wished he could even take a decent picture. But he wasn't an artist. Not in the traditional sense.

His medium was food. The sight and smell, the taste and texture, of it.

Of her.

He breathed her in, the smell of lemon icing mixing with her own unique scent that always reminded him of long, lazy mornings in bed. He thought about licking the smooth, tangy sweetness from her warm skin, the same shade as rich buttercream. His mouth watered as he stared at the delectably bold, vibrant colors she always favored now piped all over her meringue-toned body in sweet swirls.

Why this?

Because *this* was how he saw her. A work of art. A feast for the senses. A decadent wonder, meant to be savored.

But he didn't know how to say that to her. How to make her hear him and not all the other voices the told her otherwise. "I just," he shrugged and said, "want to show you the wonder and beauty I see in you."

***

Greta turned her head to look at him.

His head was bent, trying to study her intently. But she could see him fiddle with the piping bag in his hands and his cheeks flush nervously.

I want to show you the wonder and beauty I see in you.

She wanted to believe that.

"So show me."

She took a breath and reached for the zipper of her shapewear. As she pulled it down, she could feel the secure hug of it loosen. She felt the weight of her breasts shift and fall, no longer lifted and held in ideal place. She felt the flesh of her waist settle, as the hourglass form filled out. Swallowing deeply, she sighed and discarded the cloth, her last defense. She shut her eyes, but said, "Show me."

So he did. "You are so gorgeous." Taking the piping bag, he placed the tip at her shoulder. "I love your shoulders," he told her. "They're so strong and proud." She felt him draw spirals and curls across and along them, before dipping them down over her collar bone and the tops of her breasts. "God," he said, trailing the frosting over and around the full flesh, "and your breasts. I know you've probably heard it a million times from every guy you've ever been with, but..." He shook his head and sighed. "Your breasts are amazing. Mouth-watering and tempting to the touch."

He swirled the frosting up her nipples in an artistic flourish. "Sometimes, I find myself thinking about them and..." He shrugged. "Suddenly, I can't think of anything else. Can't do anything but just dream about them. Until I can finally get my hands and," he leaned down and licked the frosting from the sugared tip, "my tongue on them, I just don't feel right."

He sucked again, groaning as he did. Greta's back arched up into his touch, her moan an echo of his. He kissed his way down her breasts, taking his time over the steep slopes. Then down her rib cage. "And, having you like this..." His voice trailed off in a hungry growl that thrilled her before his lips and tongue loved her skin. "You are beautiful." He put down the piping bag and ran his hands, worshipful and adoring, over her sides, her curves, before holding her full hips in his hands as if they were—as if she were—some kind of treasure.

Gently, he kissed her navel. "I know you don't always think so," he shook his head, as if bewildered by that, before kissing the curve of her belly, the part of her body she'd always been made to feel like this heavy, burdensome shame, so sweetly she felt tears threaten her eyes, "but I wish you would."

He nuzzled her thighs. "I wish you could see what I see. Could know what I know." He nudged her legs apart, the scratch of his stubble against her exciting. "Could feel how perfect you feel."

For a brief second, her eyes fluttered shut when he adoringly kissed her sex, his breath hot on her sensitive skin. But she didn't want to miss this. She wanted to watch. Over the rise of her belly, she saw the serene look of concentrated pleasure on his face. She felt his mouth as he lapped at her labia, teasing the full flesh with his tongue.

Her body clenched and her hips thrust up. "More." She needed more.

She heard, felt, his chuckle. The sensation rippled through her, making her body writhe, before he gave her what she needed. His tongue flicked over her clit, licking and laving. Swirling as his mouth sucked.

Fuck! That was so good. Her toes curled, the feeling of the frosting flaking off her skin somehow sexy. As if her skin and her body were literally transforming into something else through his touch. Her body twisted and she felt that sensation climb her legs, putting in her mind mythic images of mermaids shedding scales for skin or Galatea being granted life from stone. This was what his touch did to her. Made her feel like more than herself.

His warm, wet mouth breathing life and love into her heated flesh made her feel *more* like herself. "More."

With an excitement and hunger that thrilled her, he gripped her. Filling his hands with her ass, those big, capable palms a perfect fit as they gripped. He pulled her closer and feasted on her.

Yes.

***

Fuck, she was hot!

Bryan felt her cup the back of his head, her fingers tangling in his hair, and he knew she was close. He could hear it in the soft sounds that escaped her lips. She bit her lip, muffling all that sensuous noise, and pushed her hips up against his mouth, filling him with her. God, he wanted to devour her. To consume and savor the whole of her. In each flick of his tongue, every nip of his teeth and sip of his lips, he loved her. All of her. Every inch and pound.

He groaned when she gripped his hair, the strands twisting in her fist, and came against his mouth. She writhed against him as sensation struck her, making her shudder with pleasure. Her body tensed, her mound and thighs pressing into him fiercely, an intense weight against his face, before letting go into almost impossible softness. Her orgasm was so sweet as the scent, the sight, the taste, and feel of it, rich and thick, flooded his senses.

He gave her one last, long, lingering lick. He heard her moan when he kissed her; her clit, her mound, her navel, her breasts, her neck, her lips. He kissed her thoroughly, drinking in the sound of her satisfaction.

It hadn't gone quite the way he'd planned. He'd wanted to cover her body in a lush buttercream garden of his own making. Wanted to transform her into a piece of edible art.

But he couldn't quite bring himself to regret a moment of the experience. It'd been better than he'd imagined. Better than anything he could have fantasized or dreamed. Because it'd been real. Realized. Not something sheltered and shuttered in the back of his brain, but something alive and shared with Greta.

Besides, that just meant he had a goal for next time. He couldn't wait.

He laughed, looking at her sprawled, sated, on the table's surface. Smeared swirls of sugared color painted the long, lush canvas of her legs. An arm lay exhausted over her frosted breasts and belly, the rise and fall of her full chest a masterpiece in motion. A Goddess at Rest. Decadence in Repose. The Taste of Temptation.

Grinning at that thought, he grabbed her hands and pulled her, limp and lazy, upright on the table's edge. "Why don't you head upstairs and take a shower?"

She blinked blankly and frowned. "What about you?"

Bryan shrugged and grabbed the discarded piping bags. "I'll clean up and join you." He picked up her discarded shirt and pants, and smiled at the idea of walking into the hazy fog of the shower, parting the curtain, and seeing her covered in nothing but soapy suds and surrounded by steam. Another lovely image.

She shook her head and took the clothes he handed her. "I mean," she said, gesturing to his hard-on, "what about you?"

He smiled and touched her nose, leaving a line of frosting there. "Don't you remember?" He laughed at her chuckle as she waved his hands away. He leaned in and licked the frosting off her face before kissing her lips. Sweet, silly, sexy girl. "This," tonight, this moment, his fantasy-come-to-life, *"was* for me."

About the Author

Sonni de Soto has two BDSM erotica novels published and stories in The New Smut Project's, The First Annual Geeky Kink's, and The Sexy Librarian's anthologies. She is a recovering Catholic who may not have held onto the beliefs she was raised with over the years between First Communion and kink parties, but still finds great meaning and reverence in ritual. Such as her first play party, that opened with a transgressive nun role play scene between two giggling pregnant women that should have felt obscene but was somehow transcendentally joyful. While she may have fallen from faith, she still firmly believes that grace may be found in a multitude of ways.

CHASMOPHILIA
by Arden de Winter

ISLA KNELT BEFORE THE ENTRANCE to Selkirk Cave, loose gravel and grit digging into the tender territory below her padded knees. The grace of a Pacific Northwest fall had left the area wet with rain; the cave's less than two-by-two foot hole sunk inches deep amid the spreading seas of an icy puddle.

She let out a long sigh and ran a gloved hand over her flannel shirt and jeans. She should've brought something that would wick away moisture, not leave her a cold, shivering mess. A more experienced caver would've known to wear a wetsuit, or at least to pack a warm change of clothes. Yet another reason Isla should turn around right now, hike back to her car, and drive home.

It was dangerous to be here alone, near suicide not to tell anyone where she'd gone. Those were the two cardinal rules for all cavers, and Isla was breaking them. She shouldn't be doing this; she knew better. Not only was it idiocy, it was wrong.

More than wrong, it was immoral.

But, even as the thought filtered across her brain, her heartbeat quickened; the delicious throb of heat that'd bloomed between her legs when she'd arrived now warred with the puddle's cold waters. An unquenchable need had driven her here to the foothills of the mountain. A desperate hunger would see her inside.

The cave opening yawned, black and hollow, crouched flat and low against its base of slate-gray stone. Despite its tight opening, what really kept Selkirk off most locals' maps was the fifteen or so feet of a tight pinch one had to crawl through in order to get to the cave proper. This keyhole entrance guaranteed that only the most experienced — or foolhardy — tested their skills here.

It would also ensure Isla some much needed privacy. On the flip side, it would mean that if she did get into trouble, no one would be coming along to find her. She'd be on her own.

The story of her life.

Isla grabbed her small pack and shoved it into the crevice. She followed after, the light from her helmet torch illuminating little beyond the foot or so of uneven rock and cramped crawlway directly in front of her. She dug padded knees into the loose gravel and mud that comprised the cave's opening and pushed deeper inside; protrusions of sharp stone biting into her back and flattening her onto her stomach.

The world shrank into a jagged throat of gray stone. Juts of rock gouged into her, an overabundance of breast and hips complicating the dimension of the tight squeeze.

Isla inched forward, her helmeted head not enough protection against the rasp of basalt as it snagged at strands of her burnished hair.

Isla shifted, bringing her front fully against the cave floor. Damp rock scraped against soft flesh; the icy rasp of rain-soaked stone and earth slickening her front and back. Where basalt met skin, goosebumps erupted; her nipples as hard as the rock she ground them against as she moved herself along, inch by inch.

She leaned into the painful caress, arching her pelvis into the ready earth. Her breasts rubbed across the unforgiving rock as she squirmed along the chilly passageway, flesh quivering with pleasure and fatigue; a heady dichotomy of sensations.

The impossible weight of tons upon tons of stone and earth pressed down on her, heavy and insistent. Grinding into her. Grinding her down.

Like a demanding lover.

Her heart pounded; Isla's panted breaths tight and shallow as her ribcage fought against the unyielding walls of the crawlway. Stale, shiftless cave air sluiced silt across the back of her tongue as she choked on tiny flecks of gravel; lungs burning with the torment of too short a breath.

Her vision danced, tiny pinpricks of light swirling before her. Yet, even as her heart hammered in her chest, the rest of her body exulted. Fear quickened her pulse, but it was something else, entirely, that found her own entrance slick and ready.

Isla's headlamp bounced off of the dimension of her bag—and the never-ending walls of stone—ahead of her, the way out an eternity of miles behind her feet. How long had she been inching her way forward? How much longer still until she reached the end?

Outstretched hands quested for an end to the claustrophobic tunnel, their gloved fingers finding only the impossible continuation of cold, wet rock. She couldn't remember the path being this long before. Had there been some cave-in, a sudden fall of loose boulders that'd blocked the way? If she couldn't push forward, would she be able to back her way out?

One final shove at her bag and she felt it push free of the cramped tunnel and into the larger chamber beyond. Isla squeezed through the last of the pinch, generous hips scraping hard along the rock walls in an effort to be free. Isla winced, the territory below her waist tender and stinging. She sighed, happy at least to be through some of the worst of it. She damn sure wasn't looking forward to going back through it on her way out.

There was a reason it was locally known as The Birth Canal.

Isla straightened her helmet and glanced across the space. Comprised mostly of basalt—and its igneous cousin andesite—the gray-on-gray tones glimmered dully in the light of her headlamp. Clusters of quartz chips blinked from the high, domed walls of the chamber, captured in that shiftless sky like tiny, frozen constellations.

Caught in the suddenness of false day, a family of drowsy bats shuddered their wings against the violation of unruly light. Isla dropped her gaze, leaving the colony in relative peace. It was best not to disturb the locals.

Cool cave air licked across Isla's damp clothes. She shivered: the near-constant cave temperature sat just above fifty degrees. The only source of heat seemed to be between her legs; her core heavy and languid after such a tough crawl.

A decent-sized, flat boulder claimed most of the center of the chamber, its larger brother step-laddering up along one wall face. If a person squinted just right, the rocks almost resembled a coffee table and couch respectively, and lent the space its locally-known name: The Parlor.

Isla reached down and slung her pack across her back. She hiked to the far side of the chamber, steps slow and careful as she navigated the damp, loose rock beneath her feet. From somewhere nearby, the sound of running water could be heard; the musty, unmoving air of the cave redolent with the earthy scent of damp mushrooms and bat guano.

A steep incline soon dominated Isla's thoughts. The last time she'd been here, one of the fellows in her caver club had misjudged a step, slipped backwards, and gotten a pretty bad sprain. If she wasn't careful, she could end her journey when it'd barely started.

The bit of a climb truncated at something of a small platform; the wide, open space beyond defying the inquisitive brightness of her headlamp. Isla knelt, dug through her pack for her second light source—a small, clip-on lamp meant to dangle from her waist—and affixed it to one of the loops of her jeans. With a little flip of a switch, bright, clean light washed the chamber in a renewed brilliance.

Isla looked around. A chill rippled across her clammy flesh at the sight of the narrow pathway ahead and the depthless chasm beside it. At only a foot or so wide it was known as The Widow's Walk, for obvious reasons. Across the brief respite of the level surface, a steep slope plummeted some thirty-five into the hidden chamber below. The gambit of rock looked deceptively straightforward from the relative ease of the platform. It was only when attempting to navigate it that one realized the treachery of that assumption.

Isla splayed her right hand high against the cave's wall where small, out-jutting daggers of stone allowed for some semblance of a handhold. Was it the numbness of her fingers that found the basalt surprisingly warm? A perversion of sensation that urged her to let her touches linger across the cave's intimate dimensions?

She gripped the shelves of rock, making sure to maintain three points of contact with the terrain, for safety. Not that following that rule would help her much if she truly lost her balance and took a tumble into the lightless ravine below. She swiveled her head and glanced over her left shoulder, down into the dark crevice. Might put a good spin on her, though, as she fell into eternal blackness; her body never to be recovered.

She sighed. Those kinds of thoughts were not helpful. But despite her eagerness—the slickened readiness dripping further down her thighs with every stride she took—the isolation was starting to get to her.

What few sounds she could hear were exaggerated, their origins difficult to pinpoint. What couldn't be heard made a kind of sound all its own, almost like a shushing whisper. In the fragile swell of her artificial halo of light, her ears strained to make sense of the nothing; sometimes supplying stimulation of their own.

Her senses hummed; a high-pitched sort of thing. As tempting as her phone was—nestled deep within her bag, memory card packed with music—she couldn't plug in. It was just too dangerous to rob herself of her hearing.

Still, it would have been nice to not feel so alone. It was strange. Isla wouldn't have thought such a thing would bother her—she'd been alone most of her adult life—yet the stark reality of her situation almost overwhelmed her. Bereft of another living soul for miles and miles around, the cave's Stygian darkness swelled round her like a burial shroud.

There was still time to turn back, even now. She'd not taxed too much of her strength getting here. Isla could easily navigate herself out of the cave and drive home, maybe swing by somewhere and pick up a hot chocolate on the way. This whole trip could be chalked up to simple misguided sexual curiosity; a desperate perversion that'd seen a young woman momentarily disregard her better judgment.

But, even as she thought it, Isla dismissed the idea. She'd come too far to turn back now. If nothing else, she wanted to see it to the end. Needed to. Some urges could not be so easily ignored.

She made her way across the Widow's Walk, shuffling first one foot across the level stone and then the other; never fully stepping off the solid ground as she made her slow way forward. The impossible openness of the ravine yawned over her shoulder; the urge to turn and gaze into the dimensionless pit was near-impossible to ignore.

Wet silt slickened the pathway underfoot. Isla shifted forward, eager to be off the ridge. Her boots slid over a particularly damp patch and she slipped.

Her world lurched. Cold fingers of fear clenched round her heart like a vice. There was a soul-shivering moment where she felt herself tip backward towards the pit. She let out a startled cry, the sound bouncing back at her from all directions. Her hands flailed desperately for purchase.

A protrusion of rock was suddenly beneath her grasp. Isla gripped the limb of stone, used it as an anchor point to shift her fall towards the safety of the rock wall. She tumbled, landing hard on padded knees; shoulder burning from the violent motion.

Isla didn't stop shaking until she'd crawled her way down, staying on her ass as much as possible, the thirty or so feet to the chamber below. She couldn't stop the shaking until she sprawled against the security of the cave floor. Her heart raced, slamming painfully against her ribcage; her panted breaths making swirling eddies of the nearby cave silt.

She should be dead: a victim to gravity and her own stupid assurance that all would be well. If she'd ended it here, no one would ever know what'd happened to her. It'd almost be as if she'd never existed at all.

Isla imagined the quiet chaos of Monday morning, when her disappearance would only be noticed once the phone system resembled an ever-blinking display of Christmas tree lights and an entire IT floor's worth of coffee pots sat forlorn, cold, and empty. Even if her boss tried to ring her, she'd never get through. There was no cell service below 40 feet of solid rock.

If it hadn't been for that handhold...

Isla clenched her fist, the same one that'd latched fast onto the rock to keep her from falling down the crevice. Thinking back on it now, she couldn't say whether she'd found the stone that'd saved her life. Or if, maybe, *it'd found her*.

The thought sobered her, and she sat up. Stale adrenaline had made a sour, curdled mess of her stomach; the subsequent crash of its absence leaving her shaky and dizzy. She dug around in her pack, hands clumsy with the last vestiges of fear. Isla grabbed her bottle of water and the baggie of trail mix, forcing herself to gulp down some of each until the terrible, hollowed-out feeling started to subside.

She looked around. Pale lamplight danced across dozens of tiny, vein-like rivulets of quartz which darted through the nearby cave wall in a well-packed, layered formation. The Mille-Feuille chamber was considered by many to be the prize of Selkirk. It was here that Isla had first fallen in love.

How could anyone not be overwhelmed at the mountain's hidden secret? It was like discovering something precious and new about someone she'd thought she'd already known through and through. Isla sighed, slow and deep, breathing in the heavy breath of the cave; the mountain's own exhalations trapped in this perfect, crystalline place. She took him in, filling herself with his essence.

Was it really so strange for someone to fall in love like that? Tahoma had been there all of her life. It'd overlooked each and every one of her triumphs, as well as her mistakes. The majestic, multi-peaked mountain had been a steady, constant presence as far back as Isla could remember.

Could anyone ask for a more devoted lover than that?

Even here, amid his foothills, Isla could feel Tahoma's timeless presence. The steady assurance of his basalt flesh. The rough danger of his forbidden affection.

That's why she'd come here today. To be as close to him as she could get. To be a vessel at his disposal. To open herself up to the impossible divine, and touch something of his glory.

She was merely one link in a long chain stretching back into antiquity, a member of a once highly-respected tradition of powerful seers who'd journeyed deep into caves in search of wisdom. In ancient Greece these were the oracles, a group of priestesses whose insights often led nations. Nowadays, scientists believed it was the hallucinogenic cave gases—or the sensory deprivation of severe isolation—which had given the oracles their mystical insights. But Isla believed it was more.

Something much more.

The sound of trickling water pulled at Isla's notice. She forced herself to focus on it, letting the sound rise to the forefront of her awareness. What'd once been a whisper grew until it dominated the small space of the chamber. Her senses vibrated, like a tuning fork, to the cave's resonance.

Frozen rivers of quartz pulsed with a steady glow, the rhythm slow and regular. Isla stood on shaky legs—the air higher-up noticeably thinner than that which blanketed the cave floor—and followed the sound. There, in a corner of the chamber, tucked behind a large boulder, was a small stream.

Isla knelt where the floor slanted into the waters, the veins of quartz in the walls now thrumming in time with her speeding pulse. Her head swam, dizzy in the throes of the cave's heartbeat. She placed a gloved hand in the waters, surprised to find them warm. Much more than warm; almost hot.

There'd not been a stream here when her caving club had come through before. Had it formed, somehow, in the few weeks since she'd last been here? Could such a thing even happen?

The water-filled trench scored into the area from a hidden system, somewhere beyond the chamber. Light from her headlamp illuminated a few feet down the drowned passage before being overshadowed by the nearby cave wall. Whether the stream ran for only a few feet before opening up somewhere nearby, or not, was anyone's guess. But Isla wouldn't leave until she'd found out. She couldn't.

Isla dropped her pack from her back, taking her time to slip out of her cold, wet clothes. She took off her helmet and unbound her dirt-streaked ponytail, easing into the bath-like waters. The stream lapped against her cold body, warming it; something of an eddy pulling her towards the nearby wall. Isla crouched and stretched out onto her belly, the hot stream enveloping her naked flesh in a kind of insistent appeal. Her tired muscles started to relax, the water's steamy vapors licking across her face like blown kisses.

The low ceiling of the stream's tunnel pressed hard against the trickling waters. If Isla hoped to squeeze down the passage, she'd have to rely on the chance of air pockets trapped beneath the stone roof and the stream. Even then, she'd probably be sucking spiders as she gulped from the inch or so of ready air she found there. Or, worse, she might find no air at all.

From somewhere in the back of her head, a warning sounded. But what was the saying? Only the rocks lived forever?

Isla took a deep breath and then propelled herself

down the darkened tunnel. The sensation of moving water glided past her face, bare fingers tender as they scraped along the stream's bottom for purchase. She kept her head down, arms reaching out blindly for handholds, legs stretched long and straight behind her.

Her back scraped across the cool ceiling, but where rough stone met naked flesh sensations quickened. Fingers of rock tickled from shoulder to the small of her back, seeming to linger across the peak of her ass as she pushed along. When the passage shrank down, warm, heavy breasts rubbed along the stream's bottom. Layers of silt and rounded pebbles caressed her flesh with a keen insistence.

Her lungs started to burn, tiny explosions of light rioting across the dark curtain of her closed eyes. Isla swiveled, bringing her face up towards the ceiling. But where lips pressed close to the rock, only more water was found.

Icy fear scoured her mind. She panicked. Isla thrashed against the unforgiving stone, outstretched fingers desperate to find an end to the tunnel. She kicked now, using her knees and feet to frantically crawl further down the stream. She had to be reaching the end of it soon. She had to be.

Darkness swelled around the edges of her sight, her system screaming for respite. Isla's stomach clenched, a sickening chill sweeping through her body.

And then she was free, pushing clear of the cramped passage. Warm, fragrant air beckoned to her and she gulped down desperate lungfuls of the stuff, growing dizzy on the simple blessing of breath.

Isla stood, but bent-double, coughing and panting for air as she wiped the water out of her eyes. When she opened them, she gasped. Soft, honeyed light radiated from the chamber's limestone walls, the normal slate-gray of Selkirk's stone giving way to the impossibility of warm, wheat-colored rock.

"This shouldn't be here," Isla whispered to herself, straightening up as she stepped out of the stream. Her voice sounded flat, hollow somehow; taken into the hungry stone like a stolen kiss.

The chamber arched some twenty or so feet above, spreading out to claim a largish, room-sized space that sat cleared of any loose stone. The walls near-vibrated with a palpable intensity, thrumming with a forbidden potency that quickened heat to Isla's core.

But what demanded her attention was the natural dais at the center of the chamber. A broken stalagmite speared out of the stone; a strange geological anomaly forming a bulbed head at the apex of the shaft. There was no other way to describe the improbable fixture: Tahoma's phallus erupted, hard and eager, from the very limestone itself.

Isla approached the centerpiece, fingers desperate to touch the warm, rigid stone. She knelt at its base, awestruck, and ran eager hands up and down the inflexible shaft. The rasp of sun-kissed limestone tickled beneath her touch, almost effervescent in the way the stone seemed to tremble in readiness.

A hot flush bloomed against Isla's cheeks; her core heavy and aching. The warmth of the room escalated, or maybe that was just the dewy heat building inside. She passed her hand over the head of the stalagmite, surprised to find the blood-warm stone soft—almost polished—at the top.

Ready.

And waiting.

Isla stood and centered herself over the mountain's phallus. She swayed back and forth against the tip of the limestone, rubbing the swollen lips of her labia in time with the cave's pulsating light. Sensation quickened inside her, a tender desperation building deep within. Soon the stalagmite's head grew wet, the massive bulb slick with her own juices.

Isla eased atop the shaft. She took Tahoma's cock inside her, the rigid form of his unyielding stone filling up her empty cavern with an impossible spear of hot limestone. A tiny, thankful sigh shuddered out of her, the feeling of being stretched full as close to peace as she'd ever known.

She threw her head back as she took in the full of the mountain, wet strands of hair licking across the ample curves of her ass cheeks. Her breath caught in her throat, the feeling of rightness impossible to ignore.

It'd been so long, so damned long! Desperate tears licked at the corners of her eyes. But just tasting of what Tahoma so willingly offered wasn't enough. She needed more of him.

She needed all of him.

Her legs shuddered, muscles shaking with fatigue and furtive eagerness. Rough stone pressed hard against the sensitive keyhole of her cervix and she eased up, rising ever so slightly up the shaft but never separating fully from Tahoma's obvious need.

The pink, slickened walls of her vulva became a sacrifice as she ground against the mountain's root, soft flesh rasped raw by the shaft of harsh, unpolished stone. Timeless grit tore into her core, a stinging castigation Isla welcomed, over and over again. Her flesh stung; a deep pain so near pleasure it continued to fuel her torrid quest towards epiphany.

The room shuddered, a seething quiver of sedimentary stone. Sweat bloomed across Isla's forehead and along the tensed territory of her upper back as she impaled herself upon the porous rock. Her heartbeat quickened; the dais rumbling beneath her in an undulating surge of immeasurable energy.

Her body trembled, Tahoma's cock pressing insistently against the soft shallow of her deep pleasure. Isla closed her eyes against the riot of sensation, a terrible blessing of rapture forming inside her core.

Faster and faster, Isla surrendered herself to the divine act. The edges of her reality blurred, the warm, bright chamber losing its defined dimensions. Isla's sense of the here and now fractured; the rock beneath her surging upward. Far below, continental plates pressed together in a final, massive, tectonic thrust of eonian elation.

An intense up-swell of magma grew behind Tahoma's stone shaft before exploding upward, its sensual heat sending Isla cascading into the abyss of her orgasm. Violent sensation consumed her, her soft, inner flesh a mess of ever-expanding contractions that violated the boundaries between herself and the mountain. She was undone, scattered in fragments of flesh and memory across the massive expanse of the entire mountain range.

In her near-delirium, Isla glimpsed the hidden universe within the earth where, close to its heart, the secret of the divine slumbered. Hidden. Yet even as she came back to herself—to the cool, basalt majesty of the Mille-Feuille chamber—Isla knew that she'd find her way back to that ecstasy someday. She had to.

Some pressures were just too great to deny.

About the Author

Arden de Winter's writing explores the dark and messier facets of love. At a young age, Arden fell for fog-choked moors, moonlit nights in ancient forests, and brooding characters. Love became a crucible, a twist of torture and delight. Arden ventures into the depths of human desire, romance, and sexuality with characters defined by their wounds and afflictions. Passion and madness blur sweet romance and obsession into fervent love. Arden also writes under S.B. Roark.

**And if you loved this anthology,
please leave a review!**

MORE ABOUT SINCYR PUBLISHING

At SinCyr Publishing, we wish to provide relatable characters facing real problems to our readers, in the sexiest or most romantic manner possible. Our intent is to offer a large selection of books to readers that cover topics ranging from sexual healing to sexual empowerment, to body positivity, gender equality, and more.

Too many of us experience body shaming, sexual shaming, and/or sexual abuse in our lives and we want to publish stories that allow people to connect to the characters and find healing. This means showing healthy BDSM practices, characters that understand consent and proper communication, characters that stare down toxic culture and refuse to take part… No matter what the content is, our focus is on empowering our readers through our books.